Sweeping Doctor Steinberg behind him, Data caught one of his opponent's wrists and whipped him toward a bulkhead. . . .

Bracing himself for the attack of two other creatures, he fended off the first of them with a backhanded smash. The other managed to get a sharp-clawed grip on his arm.

The android was about to take hold of the lizard-being by the scruff of its scaly neck and fling it away, when he was filled with a sensation unlike any he'd ever known. A powerful electrical charge was running through him, savaging the workings of his neural net, disrupting his most basic functions.

Even as Data sank to his knees, no longer in control of his own limbs, he realized that the electrical emis sion had come from the creature holding on to his arm.

Taking note of his helplessness, another creature jumped him. And another. Unable to defend himself, he could only watch as they tore at his containment suit and speculate as to what would happen when they got past it and began tearing at *him*. . . .

Star Trek: The Next Generation
STARFLEET ACADEMY

Star Trek: Deep Space Nine

Star Trek movie tie-in

Star Trek Generations

Available from MINSTREL Books

STAR TREK
THE NEXT GENERATION®

STARFLEET ACADEMY™ #7

THE SECRET OF THE LIZARD PEOPLE

Michael Jan Friedman

**Interior illustrations by
Todd Cameron Hamilton**

A MINSTREL® BOOK

PUBLISHED BY POCKET BOOKS

New York   London   Toronto   Sydney   Tokyo   Singapore

A MINSTREL PAPERBACK *ORIGINAL*

A Minstrel Book published by
POCKET BOOKS, a division of Simon & Schuster Inc.
1230 Avenue of the Americas, New York, NY 10020

STAR TREK is a Registered Trademark of Paramount Pictures.

This book is published by Pocket Books, a division of Simon & Schuster Inc., under exclusive license from Paramount Pictures.

ISBN: 0-671-50109-7

First Minstrel Books printing April 1995

10 9 8 7 6 5 4 3 2 1

A MINSTREL BOOK and colophon are registered trademarks of Simon & Schuster Inc.

Cover art by Catherine Huerta

Printed in the U.S.A.

For Jake, our newest Trekker

STARFLEET TIMELINE

2264

The launch of Captain James T. Kirk's five-year mission, _U.S.S. Enterprise,_ NCC-1701.

2292

Alliance between the Klingon Empire and the Romulan Star Empire collapses.

2293

Colonel Worf, grandfather of Worf Rozhenko, defends Captain Kirk and Doctor McCoy at their trial for the murder of Klingon chancellor Gorkon.

Khitomer Peace Conference, Klingon Empire/Federation (_Star Trek VI_).

2323

Jean-Luc Picard enters Starfleet Academy's standard four-year program.

2328

The Cardassian Empire annexes the Bajoran homeworld.

2341

Data enters Starfleet Academy.

2342

Beverly Crusher (née Howard) enters Starfleet Academy Medical School, an eight-year program.

2346

Romulan massacre of Klingon outpost on Khitomer.

2351

In orbit around Bajor, the Cardassians construct a space station that they will later abandon.

2353

William T. Riker and Geordi La Forge enter Starfleet Academy.

2354

Deanna Troi enters Starfleet Academy.

2356

Tasha Yar enters Starfleet Academy.

2357

Worf Rozhenko enters Starfleet Academy.

2363

Captain Jean-Luc Picard assumes command of U.S.S. Enterprise, NCC-1701-D.

2367

Wesley Crusher enters Starfleet Academy.
An uneasy truce is signed between the Cardassians and the Federation.
Borg attack at Wolf 359; First Officer Lieutenant Commander Benjamin Sisko and his son, Jake, are among the survivors.
U.S.S. Enterprise-D defeats the Borg vessel in orbit around Earth.

2369

Commander Benjamin Sisko assumes command of Deep Space Nine in orbit over Bajor.

Source: Star Trek® Chronology / Michael Okuda and Denise Okuda

THE SECRET OF THE LIZARD PEOPLE

CHAPTER

1

"Super-Jovian planet ignition," said the Academy instructor, a man named Pritchard, whose jug-handle ears were each almost as large as his narrow, bony face. "What is it? And why should we care?"

Without the slightest hesitation, Data raised his hand. His friend Sinna, who was sitting next to him in the Academy's large, semicircular lecture hall, looked at him and rolled her eyes. No doubt, it seemed to her that he was *always* the first one to come up with an answer— despite the relative obscurity of the subject.

Then again, Data was an android, with a positronic brain capable of storing as much information as a fair-sized computer. So it should have come as no surprise to his fellow cadets that he knew a few more things than they did.

"Mr. Data," said Pritchard, taking notice of the android's raised hand. "I see that you, at least, are as

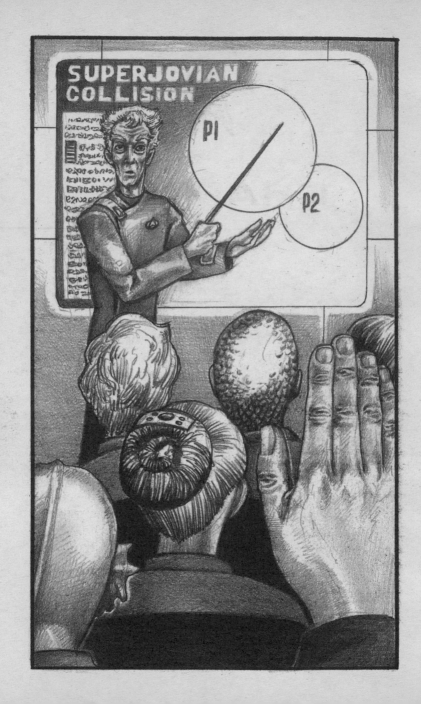

prepared as ever." He cleared his throat. "Well, then?"

"Super-Jovian planet ignition," Data declared, "is a process that involves a pair of gas-giant planets on a collision course. One of these bodies must be at least seventy-five times the mass of Jupiter, the other ten or more times Jupiter's mass. When such worlds come together with sufficient impact, the greater of the two may grow heavy enough to begin fusion and become a new, small star."

The instructor nodded approvingly. "Yes. Exactly right. And of what significance is this to *us?*"

This time there were a number of hands, Sinna's among them. But Pritchard's gaze remained fixed on Data.

"Go on," he told the android.

Sinna grunted softly. The streaks that ran from her temples, behind her ears, and down her neck turned an even deeper shade of blue—further evidence of her frustration. Ignoring his friend, Data provided the response required of him.

"As Starfleet officers," he explained, "we may encounter this phenomenon or something similar. At such a time, it will be our responsibility to recognize what is happening and to record it with the appropriate array of sensor instruments. Moreover, a super-Jovian ignition may cause gravitic aberrations in space, creating hazards for starships . . . and also for planetary populations in the same solar system."

The instructor smiled. "Very good, Mr. Data. Very good, indeed. And you will be glad to learn that there will soon be a chance for you to put your theoretical knowledge to the test."

The android looked at Pritchard and shook his head. "No, sir," he said. "I will not be."

The instructor's smile faded a bit. "I don't think you understand what I'm telling you," he persisted. "You see, you and everyone else in this room have been selected to take part in the examination of a super-Jovian planet ignition. A *real* one, mind you, not a holographic recreation. Starfleet is taking the *Republic* out of mothballs for the occasion ... so you can all get some deep-space experience under your belts."

All around Data, cadets were grinning and nudging each other enthusiastically. Sinna seemed pleased as well. But the android could not take part in their celebration.

Nor could he allow Pritchard's remark to go uncorrected. "I am *not* glad to learn of the activity you have described," said Data.

The instructor looked at him, his wispy eyebrows pinching together. "And why is that?" he inquired.

"As an android," he explained, "I am incapable of gladness, just as I am incapable of sorrow, anger, or affection. In fact, I am incapable of any emotion at all."

Pritchard sighed and folded his arms across his chest. "Ah, yes. Yes, of course. I am familiar with your troubles in that regard, Mr. Data. I assure you . . . when I said *glad,* I intended it only as a figure of speech."

The android tilted his head slightly—a habit of his when engaged in an attempt to comprehend human behavior. "I see," he responded. Understanding spoken language would be so much easier, he mused, if people would only say what they really *meant*.

Recognizing idioms had been a particular problem for him since his arrival at the Academy nearly three weeks ago. Indeed, he had been here less than an hour before a fellow cadet generously advised him to "pull up a chair."

Data had done exactly as the cadet had suggested. It was only after his action was followed by a round of uproarious laughter that Sinna offered him an explanation. It seemed "pull up a chair" was jargon for "sit down." Again, a case where humans perversely refused to speak in precise terms.

Back on the *Tripoli*, the Starfleet ship that had discovered him in the Omicron Theta system three years earlier, he had had little contact with any crewman but Captain Thorsson. And Thorsson was always careful to use words the android could not misunderstand.

Even after his departure from the *Tripoli*, his experience with biological beings had been limited. As a result, he was almost totally unprepared for the onslaught of quirky and unfamiliar words and phrases that the other cadets seemed to employ on a constant basis.

Unfortunately, this did not work to enhance Data's chances of being accepted among them. After the "chair" incident, the other cadets appeared to see him as someone different, someone apart—and therefore, to avoid him whenever possible. It was a pity, he thought. After all, he had come to the Academy seeking the companionship of what he believed were his peers.

Perhaps when one was an artificial life-form, he thought, one could have no peers. Except Sinna, of course. And hers was a most unusual case.

Data had met Sinna on the transport vessel bearing both of them to the Academy. She was one of four Yann who had been accepted into that year's freshman class.

Since the Yann were a clannish race, given to congregating in groups and depending too much on one another's support, the Academy administrators had seen fit to separate Sinna and her companions as much as possible. Apparently, this was perfectly acceptable to Sinna, who had acquired a measure of independence through her association with the android.

It was a good thing for Data, too. Without Sinna, he would have had no friends here at all.

"Well, then," said Pritchard, "I believe that's all the time we have for today. But if you're smart, you'll study up on the phenomenon you're about to witness out in space." He turned to the android. "Except for you, of course, Mr. Data. You obviously know all you need to know about super-Jovian planet ignitions ... and just about everything else."

The android inclined his head ever so slightly. "Thank you," he told the instructor—even though he knew Pritchard was wrong.

There were many things he didn't know—things that came as easily as breathing to all the other cadets. And at times, he wondered if he would *ever* be clever enough to learn them.

It wasn't long before Data, Sinna, and the rest of their Academy contingent were beamed up to the starship *Republic* and shown to their quarters by the vessel's skeleton crew. The idea was that with some fifty cadets aboard, only a handful of *real* officers would be needed to pilot the *Republic* and oversee the necessary experiments.

Within hours, the ship broke its orbit around Earth and took off for Beta Arantialus, the system where the super-Jovian planet in question would soon become a full-fledged star. At slightly more than warp eight, the *Republic* was slated to complete the journey in four days.

It was at an after-dinner briefing that Data learned which cadets he would be working with and what experiments they would be conducting. As it turned out, the android's subgroup would be in charge of recording certain mass-to-energy conversion ratios—as important a job as any other on this voyage.

However, that was not the news that intrigued Data the most. It was the fact that second-year cadet Glen Majors had been chosen by Captain Clark to lead the subgroup.

"You know him?" asked Sinna.

At that moment, Majors was standing on the other side of the briefing room. He was tall and athletic-looking, with thick, dark, wavy hair and a quick, easy smile. He was surrounded by several ranks of admiring first-year cadets—most of them female.

"We have never met," Data conceded. "However, I have read a great deal about him. Cadet Majors has set new records in several of the Academy's academic and physical performance categories. By all accounts, he is destined for a choice spot on one of the fleet's foremost vessels."

Sinna grunted. "Really," she said. She didn't appear to be particularly impressed.

The android, on the other hand, was determined to

meet Glen Majors. It seemed to him he could learn a
lot from such an accomplished young man.

However, before Data could carry out his intent, he
was approached by a couple of first-year cadets. One was
slender, with hair the color of ripe wheat. The other
was shorter and powerfully built, with dark eyes and a
complexion to match.

The android had seen both cadets in class, though he
had not been introduced to either of them. Apparently,
that was about to change.

"Hi," said the slender one, smiling warmly at both
Data and his companion. "I'm McCall. My friend here
is Piazza."

"Yes," the android responded. "I know. I have heard
various instructors refer to you by name."

Sinna just nodded her head. She didn't seem particularly enthusiastic to meet these two.

"And you're Data," noted the one called Piazza. He
fixed his dark, almost black eyes on the android.

Data was not surprised that the cadet knew him. He
was, after all, the only android in the entire Academy—
perhaps in the entire *universe*.

"In fact," he said, "I *am* Data." Remembering his
manners, he indicated his companion with a gesture.
"And this is Sinna. She is a first-year student at the
Academy as well."

The two cadets turned to the Yanna. "Pleased to meet
you, Sinna," said McCall.

Sinna eyed him. "Same here," she answered.

But even the android could tell that her heart wasn't
in it. He wondered about that.

Turning back to Data, McCall said, "They tell me you're an android. Is that true?"

"Quite true," Data confirmed.

"I've never met an android before," the human went on soberly. His brows met over the bridge of his up-turned nose. "What's it like?" he asked. And then, with even greater intensity, "Being *you*, I mean?"

As McCall completed his query, Data saw him dart a sideways glance at Piazza. Piazza glanced back.

"It is difficult to answer that question," the android replied honestly. "Having never been anyone else, I have no ready standard for comparison."

McCall nodded sagely. "I understand. Maybe I can put it another way, then." He paused, appearing to weigh his choice of words carefully. Finally, he seemed to have devised the proper phrasing. "When you get hungry, do you prefer to eat raw metals . . . or alloys? And do you prefer them *with* condiments or *without?*"

Data looked at him. Apparently, this individual knew very little about androids. But then, he was hardly alone in that regard.

"First of all," he answered, "I do not *get* hungry, though I may sometimes eat when others are eating for the sake of sociability. For the purpose of nutrition, I occasionally ingest a semiorganic nutrient suspension in a silicon-based liquid medium. However, I have never felt the need to sample either metals *or* alloys, nor do I indulge in condiments of any sort."

Piazza cleared his throat. Data glanced at him but saw that the cadet's discomfort was only momentary.

"And what about rest?" asked McCall. "You feel the need to catch a few *winks* now and then, don't you?"

"If by *winks* you are referring to sleep," the android explained, "then I do not seem to feel such a need. My systems are efficient enough that they do not require downtime. However, I could mimic sleep by slowing down my various functions . . . that is, if I were motivated to do so."

Cadet Piazza found it necessary to clear his throat again. "Sorry," he said. He looked to his companion. "Please, go ahead," he told McCall. "This is really . . . um, fascinating."

"Data . . ." interjected Sinna.

He turned to her. "Yes?"

The Yanna seemed uncomfortable, for some reason the android couldn't fathom. Taking hold of his arm, she said, "Maybe we'd better go now."

Data looked at her, a little surprised. "Go?" he echoed. "But we just—"

"I *really* think we ought to go," she urged, still hanging on to the android's arm. "I mean *now.*"

It would have been impolite for Data to refuse, given the extent of his friend's insistence. Turning to McCall and Piazza, the android did his best to look apologetic.

"It seems I must be leaving now," he told them. "Perhaps we can continue our conversation another time."

"I'd like that," said McCall, smiling understandingly. "Oh, just one more question before you go, Data. I was wondering where you get your hair cut. I wouldn't mind trying that look myself."

The android shrugged. "I have never *had* my hair cut, so I cannot advise you in that regard. You see," he clarified, "my hair only grows when I wish it to, and thus

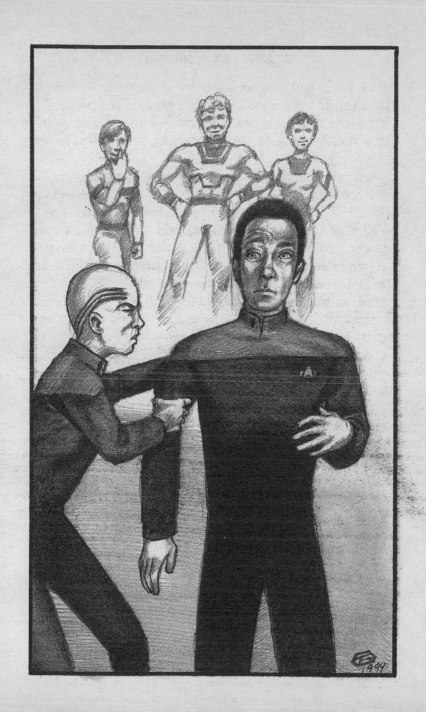

far, I have had no occasion to implement that wish. However, if I did encourage hair growth, it would—"

"Excuse me," said someone whose voice Data didn't recognize. Turning, he saw that someone new had joined the conversation.

And not just *anyone*. It was Cadet Glen Majors.

"I couldn't help but overhear what you were talking about," Majors remarked. His attention was focused only on McCall and Piazza, as if Data and Sinna weren't even present. "Maybe you two haven't been in the Academy long enough to figure out how things work around here. But if I were you, I'd wise up—and fast."

The android noticed the sudden change in the complexions of the two first-year cadets. Both McCall and Piazza had become red in the face.

"Am I making myself clear?" asked Majors.

McCall nodded. "Come on," he muttered, elbowing his companion.

"Uh huh," Piazza agreed. And a moment later, the two of them had slunk off.

Majors turned to Data and Sinna. "Sorry about that," he told them. "Some people get their kicks needling others." Glancing back over his shoulder at the clutch of first-year cadets he'd been conversing with, he winked. "Fortunately," he continued, in a somewhat louder voice, "you won't see too much of that by the end of your first year. By then, all the practical jokers have been weeded out."

The android was beginning to understand now. McCall and Piazza had been having fun at his expense—a situation Sinna had apparently recognized, which was the reason she had wished him to withdraw from the conversation.

Majors had recognized the situation as well, it seemed, and intervened on Data's behalf. The android was pleased by the second-year cadet's involvement, though he could not have said exactly why that should be.

"Thank you," Data told Majors. "I—"

But Majors hadn't waited to hear the end of the android's statement. He was already on his way back to the group of first-year students he had been addressing earlier.

"Come on," said Sinna. "Let's go back to our quarters, Data."

But the android didn't want to leave. He wished to wait until Majors completed his exchange with the other cadets and then attempt to thank him again.

"I said come *on*," the Yanna repeated. And pulling on his arm, she guided him out of the briefing room.

CHAPTER

It wasn't until they were out in the corridor and quite alone that Sinna turned to Data and snorted angrily. "Sweet deities," she fumed, "couldn't you see what was going on in there?"

The android could only stare at her. Back on the *Yosemite,* the vessel that had brought him and the Yann to Earth, he and Sinna had risked their lives together. In the course of those events, he had seen her look afraid, resolute, and finally triumphant.

But he had never seen her so positively *incensed.*

"Of course," he said. "Cadets McCall and Piazza were ridiculing me—though I did not realize it at first. Cadet Majors intervened and caused them to stop—which is why I wanted to stay and find an opportunity to thank him properly."

Sinna rolled her eyes. "Data... Majors stopped McCall and Piazza, all right—and I'm glad he did. But he wasn't doing it for *you*. He was doing it to impress those other first-year cadets."

"I do not understand," the android said. Truthfully, he didn't. He recalled Majors's words verbatim—not a difficult task, given the capabilities of his positronic brain. But he still didn't see his friend's point.

"In fact," he remarked, "I was pleased that Cadet Majors took such an interest in me. I believe I can only benefit from even a casual association with such an exemplary student."

Sinna stopped in the middle of the corridor and turned to Data. "All right," she told him. "You like Cadet Majors so much, you learn all you can from him. I promise I won't say a word about it . . . no matter what."

With that, she turned on her heel and marched down the corridor toward the turbolift. The android was certainly no expert on Yannish emotions, but it seemed to him it wouldn't be a good idea to follow Sinna at this particular time.

Instead, he stood there in the corridor for several minutes, enduring the scrutiny of other cadets and crewmen as they walked by. Then, when Data was certain he had given Sinna a sufficient head start, he entered the turbolift and asked it to take him to his solitary quarters.

All that first night on the *Republic,* Data sat in his room, pondering the details of the encounter that had led Sinna to become angry with him. By morning, he had to confess that he still didn't understand the vehemence of her reaction.

How could she have observed the same things he had . . . and come to such different conclusions about them? As

15

far as the android could tell, Cadet Majors's actions had been rather chivalrous. And if I am going to be an asset to Starfleet, Data thought, it is about time I exhibited some confidence in my own judgment.

The android found himself wishing that he were more like Glen Majors. Now *there* was someone with confidence, someone who would never second-guess himself. Someone whom it might be instructive to observe ...

And to *emulate.*

Data straightened in his chair as his course of action became clear to him. Looking up at the intercom grid hidden in the ceiling, he said, "Computer, where is Cadet Majors?"

"Cadet Majors is in the ship's gymnasium," the computer reported.

"Thank you," the android responded. If he had gleaned anything from his stay on the *Tripoli*, it was the importance of being polite.

"You are welcome," returned the computer, just as politely—though its behavior stemmed from its programming, Data reflected, not its experience.

Getting up, he headed for the door to his quarters. He would pay Glen Majors a visit in the gymnasium, he resolved. And if it were possible to *learn* confidence, he would do just that.

The *Republic*'s gymnasium was almost identical to the one Data had encountered on the *Tripoli.* It was a large, brightly lit room with a high ceiling and a great many mats strewn across the floor. In addition, there were two sets of hanging rings, a trio of leathery pommel horses, and a gleaming high bar made out of duranium.

As the android entered, he saw that Cadet Majors was hanging vertically from the high bar, with his back to him. A female cadet with long, black hair was standing off to one side, intent on Majors as he began to move— arching his back almost imperceptibly at first just to start himself swinging, and then kicking out with increasing enthusiasm at the end of each forward motion until his body was parallel to the floor at the high points of his arc.

As the female watched, Majors stepped up his efforts even more. After several seconds, he had achieved enough momentum to completely circle the bar, a feat he accomplished once ... twice ... and a third time, before finally letting go of it.

With consummate grace, the cadet somersaulted through the air and achieved a perfect landing some five meters in front of the bar. The female nodded.

"Pretty good," she said.

Majors approached her, extending his hand. "Just *pretty* good?"

As he took her hand in his, the female frowned good-naturedly. "All right," she conceded. "*Very* good."

"Come on," he continued. "Admit it. You've never seen anybody pull that off with such grace . . . such aplomb." He grinned. "And right about now, you're thinking, how can I get to know this hunk a little better?"

The female rolled her eyes. "Give me a break," she told him, slipping her hand free.

But Majors was undaunted. Leaning closer to her, so that his face was only inches from hers, he said, "Dinner tonight? Just you and me and the stars?"

17

Gazing at him, the female seemed to hesitate. Several seconds went by, and she still hadn't answered Majors's question.

Apparently, neither one of the cadets had noticed Data's entrance. It seemed to be as good a time as any to correct that situation.

"Hello," said the android, marching across the sea of mats in the direction of Glen Majors. "I witnessed your performance on the high bar, and like your companion, I believe it was very good."

Both Majors and the female stared at him for a moment, their mouths hanging open. The female was the first to shut hers.

"Data," said Majors. "What are *you* doing here?"

The android shrugged. "I wished to express my gratitude for your actions in the briefing room last night. After all, you did come to my defense."

Chuckling softly, the female cadet made her way past Data to the gymnasium exit. Seeing her go, Majors extended a hand in her direction, as if to draw her back.

"Wait," he called. "What about dinner?"

The female darted a glance back over her shoulder at him. "I just remembered," she replied, smiling. "I've got other plans."

As she left the room, Majors muttered something under his breath. The guttural quality of it rendered it impossible to make out.

"I beg your pardon?" the android responded.

Majors turned to him, frowning. "Never mind." A pause. "Listen, Data, this is a bad time to be thanking me." He glanced at the exit. "A *real* bad time. Understand?"

Data didn't understand. He said so.

The human grunted. "All right. If you wanted to thank me, you've done that. We're even, right?"

The android tilted his head to one side. "Actually, there was one other thing. I had hoped—"

Majors looked at him. "What? You'd hoped *what?*" There was a distinct note of impatience in his voice.

Data went on. "I had hoped you could teach me to be more confident."

The cadet's brow furrowed. "More . . . confident?"

The android nodded. "You see, I lack human instincts. This puts me at a disadvantage when it comes to decision-making—not just in reaching a conclusion but in having the self-assurance to carry it out."

Majors nodded. "I get the picture. And you want me to *teach* you those things?"

"Yes," said Data. "I do. What is more, I am willing to follow every step you take, from the time you wake until the time you go to sleep, if that is what it takes to improve myself in this area."

The other cadet appeared to pale for a second or two. His Adam's apple climbed the length of his throat before falling again.

"Tell you what," he answered finally. "The best way to learn confidence is from far away. From *very* far. If you watch me too closely, I'll be distracted, and then your . . . um, *data* will be flawed. You won't see the real *me.*"

The android thought about it for a moment. "It sounds as if you expect my presence to be obtrusive," he concluded. "If you do not want me to be in your way, all

19

you need do is say so. You cannot hurt my feelings. I do not have any."

Majors's eyes narrowed at the information. Abruptly, he smiled. "Well, then, I'm glad you see it that way," he said. "Now, if you don't mind . . ." He glanced meaningfully at the high bar, indicating his desire to resume his workout.

Taking the hint, Data crossed the gymnasium and made use of the exit. As the sliding doors *whooshed* closed behind him, the android reflected on his conversation with Glen Majors.

Perhaps Data would not have the opportunity to obtain advice from the second-year cadet after all. However, he could do what Majors advised: he could observe the human from afar. And if he watched Majors very carefully, he might soon achieve some portion of the self-assurance he sought.

In the days that followed, Data found that observing Cadet Majors unobtrusively was a good deal more difficult than it had first seemed. Despite his remarkable eyesight, there were few places on the *Republic* where he would have a clear view of Majors without the cadet's having a clear view of him in return.

However, the android didn't want the object of his scrutiny to feel put upon, so he did the best he could. And after a while, he got rather good at covert surveillance.

Unfortunately, he could not say that his efforts were actually teaching him anything about confidence. At least, not yet. However, even Data was aware that some things just took time.

Of course, the android could only devote a fraction of his time to the study of Glen Majors. The bulk of each day was devoted to the instruments and scales he would be using to record the super-Jovian planet ignition. And while Majors was sometimes working side by side with Data during these sessions, both of them were too absorbed in what they were doing to be aware of much else.

The android was also looking forward to learning other things. For instance, each subgroup of cadets was given a chance to man the ship's bridge for several hours. As it happened, Data's group was the last in line for this duty.

As a result, it was late on the fourth day out from Earth when the android sat down in the helmsman's chair and looked out across the bridge at the *Republic*'s main viewscreen. Glancing at his instrument panel, he noted that the ship was still proceeding at warp eight, the same speed it had achieved on leaving Earth's solar system.

However, that was bound to change—and rather soon. The Beta Arantialus system was just ahead. In fact, Data estimated, it would be necessary to slow to impulse power sometime in the next couple of minutes.

No sooner had he made that determination than he felt a hand on his shoulder. Looking up, he saw that it belonged to Captain Clark, a tall woman with long, gray-streaked, brown hair. She was smiling at him.

"You've done a good job around here," she told him. "I thought I'd let you be the one to take us down to sublight."

"Aye, sir," said the android. Making the necessary ad-

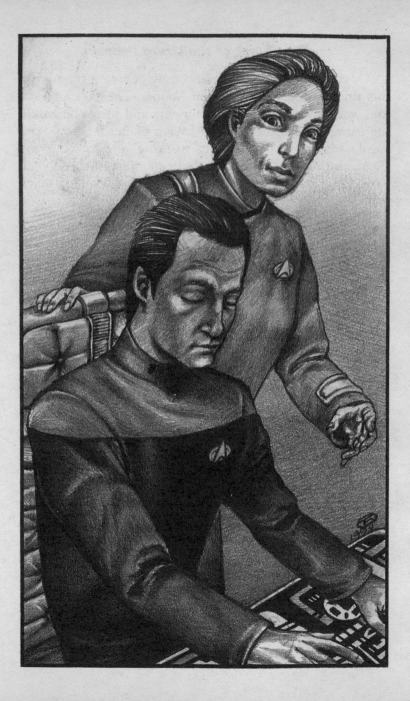

justments on his console, he did his best to comply with the captain's order. A moment later, he could see the streaks of starlight on the viewscreen diminishing in length as the ship's impulse engines took over.

"Captain?"

Data glanced over his shoulder at Cadet Petros, the petite honey-blond who had been assigned to the communications board. Like the android and Sinna, Petros was a first-year student at the Academy.

"Yes?" asked Captain Clark. "What is it, Petros?"

The cadet stared at her monitor a moment before answering, as if trying to make sure she wasn't about to embarrass herself. "I believe I'm picking up a distress signal," she said at last. "Bearing one three zero mark six, sir. At a distance of . . ." Again, she hesitated. "It looks like two point eight billion kilometers."

Cadet Majors was sitting next to Data at the navigator's console. His fingers darted across his controls with precision and dispatch. "That's just fifty million kilometers or so from the super-Jovian worlds," he concluded.

Data glanced at Sinna, who was seated at the science station, the glare of its monitors bathing her face in a green light. Then he looked at the captain. Clark was frowning slightly.

"Hail the source of the signal," she instructed Petros.

The cadet did as she was told. However, the hail produced no response other than a continuation of the distress signal. Captain Clark's frown was deepening by the minute.

First Officer Sierra, a stocky man with a thick mustache, left the bridge's command center to stand by her side. "We're the only vessel in the area," he pointed out.

"We've got to respond, even if we are on a training mission."

As the android watched, Clark nodded. "I'm well aware of that, Juan." With a single glance, she took in all four of the cadets on her bridge. "I was thinking about *them*. After all, I did promise them a shot at some bridge duty."

The first officer sighed. "Captain ..."

Clark nodded. "I know." Eyeing each cadet in turn, she expressed a silent apology. Then she said, "Sorry, people. This could be serious. I'm going to have to get some experienced officers up here."

Sinna and Petros showed varying degrees of disappointment. However, Data fully understood the reasons for her decision. Had he been in charge, he told himself, he would likely have done the same thing.

"Oh the other hand," the captain told them, "it'll be a good experience for you to see how we handle a distress-call response. You can all stand to one side of communications and look on, if you like."

Unhesitatingly speaking for all of them, Cadet Majors said, "We'd like that very much, sir."

Captain Clark shot him an approving look, with just a hint of a smirk. "Then that's where you'll go, Mr. Majors. Just remember to wait until your relief shows up."

As the android watched, Majors returned the captain's expression, as if he were sharing a private joke with her. And perhaps he was. After all, with his record, he would clearly become a captain himself some day.

"Aye, sir," replied Majors. "I'll remember."

CHAPTER
3

Though Data had seen graphic representations of asteroid belts, he had never had the opportunity to observe a real one. That is, until now.

From his vantage point next to the communications console, he could see that this particular belt was comprised of hundreds of irregularly shaped rocks, each one between a half kilometer and five kilometers in diameter. Fortunately, they were spaced far enough apart from one another to allow the *Republic* easy passage through their midst, because somewhere in this collection of orbiting debris was the source of the distress signal they had received earlier.

"Steady as she goes," cautioned Captain Clark. She had taken a couple of steps toward the viewscreen as soon as the asteroid belt became visible. Nor had she taken her eyes off it since.

Commander Sierra, who was still standing next to his

commanding officer, moved now to a spot just behind the science console. "Anything unusual?" he asked casually.

The science officer, a Pandrilite, shrugged his huge shoulders. "A fair amount of radiation emanating from some material in the asteroids," he muttered. "But nothing powerful enough to present a danger to us."

"What did he say?" Sinna wondered out loud, craning her neck to listen more closely to the officers' conversation.

"He said there was a fair amount of radiation," Data replied. "However, it does not represent a danger to us."

The Yanna looked up at him. "Thanks," she told him, frowning a little. Obviously, she had still not forgiven him for his decision to ignore her advice.

"You are welcome," he assured her.

"Be quiet," Majors whispered sharply, "or they'll tell us to leave the bridge."

The android nodded, resolving inwardly not to speak out loud unless he was required to by one of the ship's officers. After all, he did not want to be the cause of their being dismissed.

"I've got something," announced the navigator, a man with red hair and freckles who couldn't have been too long out of the Academy himself. His fingers danced over his controls. "Same bearing as the signal, and its composition is markedly different from that of these rocks."

"Can't see it yet," noted the captain. She folded her arms across her chest. "Try increasing magnification."

Everything on the viewscreen seemed to jump closer to them. And as it did, Data caught sight of what they were looking for. Tilting his head closer to Sinna's, he whispered, "There it is."

His friend looked up at him. "There *what* is?"

"Some sort of space station," he explained. "With thruster capability, if its external structures are any indication. It is partially hidden by one of the asteroids."

Sinna turned to the screen, then back to the android. "You *see* something out there? Besides all those big rocks, I mean?"

It was only then that he recalled how much more efficient his vision was than that of any biological entity. "Yes," he confirmed. "I see the station I have attempted to describe. Or more accurately, a part of it."

Majors cast a glance in Data's direction. "I told you to be *quiet*," he reminded them.

But it was too late. The captain had already turned to look at them.

"Did I hear someone mention a *station?*" she asked.

The android didn't detect any rancor in her voice, though he was hardly an expert on interpreting human gestures. In any case, he took a step forward.

"*I* mentioned a station," he admitted. He pointed to the viewscreen. "The one up there," he added.

Captain Clark's eyes narrowed ever so slightly. "You can see a station?" she asked. "When no one else can?" She paused. "Are your eyes that good, Mr. Data?"

The android nodded. "Yes, sir." It was no more than the truth. His eyes *were* that good.

A few minutes later, his observations were shown to be accurate, as the *Republic* edged nearer to its target. The source of the distress signal *was* some sort of alien space station, though they couldn't find anything like it

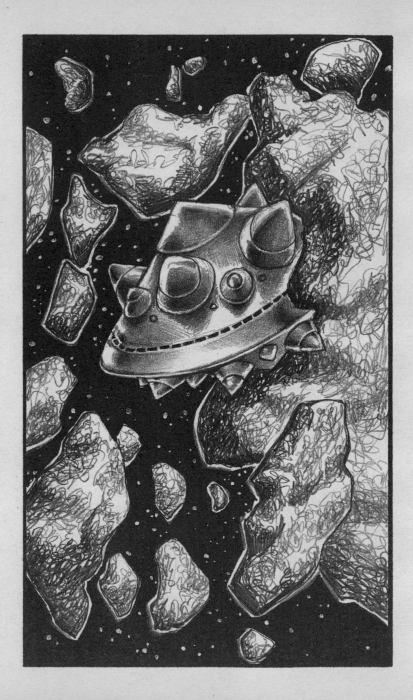

in the ship's computer files, and it had clearly crashed into one of the asteroids with which it was still entangled.

To Data, the alien structure looked like a collection of white cones sticking out at odd angles, larger ones alternating with smaller ones. Some of the cones appeared to have windows in them, while others did not. There were also several small inverted cones, which the android had assumed were the station's thrusters.

The navigator seemed to agree with the assumption. Leaning back in his chair, he said, "Looks like it was trying to negotiate this belt when its thruster array misfired. Its inertia carried it into the asteroid . . . and *boom.*"

Captain Clark turned to her science officer. "Survivors?" she asked.

He shook his head. "Impossible to say. There's too much radiation in the area. I can't even tell if any of its systems are still operable."

"No one on board answers our hails," reported the communications officer, a blond man with a neatly trimmed beard. "Either they're not receiving . . ." His voice hung ominously in the air.

"Or there's no one left alive to hear us," the captain concluded, "even though it's still sending out a signal." She scowled and turned to the science officer again. "How much time do we have before the planet's ignition?"

The super-Jovian worlds . . . Data had mentally put them aside in his preoccupation with the alien space station. He knew the answer to Captain Clark's question nearly two and a half seconds before the science officer gave it to her.

"Seven hours, sixteen minutes," replied the Pandrilite. "And when it ignites, it'll destroy this station and anyone on it, alive or otherwise."

Captain Clark bit her lip. "Is it possible for us to beam an away team over to the station so we can get some idea of what happened there?"

The science officer shook his large, blue-skinned head. "Not with all the radiation we've got here. If you want some firsthand observations, you're going to have to send a team over in a shuttle."

The captain weighed the option—her only one, apparently—for a second or two. Then she grunted.

"A shuttle it is," she decided.

"I'll get one ready," responded First Officer Sierra. "And a team as well."

He was halfway to the turbolift when Captain Clark held up her hand. "Hang on, Mr. Sierra. We can't spare experienced personnel for this purpose. I need them here with me, in case something goes wrong." She turned to Data and his colleagues. "Looks like you folks are elected. Pick up some containment suits down in ship's stores and meet Commander Sierra in Shuttlebay One."

The first officer didn't seem altogether comfortable with the idea of leading a handful of cadets. "Captain," he said, "if there *are* survivors, they'll likely need some kind of medical attention."

"Agreed," his commanding officer responded. "That's why you're going to bring Dr. Steinberg along. If there's a problem in that regard, she'll be able to handle it." Clark harrumphed. "She'd *better* be. Dr. Steinberg is about the only health care professional we've got on board."

Commander Sierra looked as if he would have liked to protest further. However, he swallowed whatever additional objections he may have had and made his way to the lift.

Data and his fellow cadets fell in behind him. Like the others, the android looked forward to the prospect of seeing what had happened on the alien station. He hoped, above all, that he wouldn't appear incompetent in the eyes of Cadet Glen Majors.

As Data and the other cadets filed into Shuttlebay One, the android reflected on how seldom he was likely to need a containment suit in his Starfleet career. After all, the alloys of which he was constructed provided protection for him against most forms of radiation, not to mention extreme heat and cold, and he was capable of going for long periods of time without oxygen.

Of course, the radiation that had disabled the alien station might be one form to which he was vulnerable. And even if radiation turned out not to be a problem, he would need a means of conversing with his fellow away team members. The containment suits' built-in communicators provided that means.

Commander Sierra was standing next to the entrance to one of the shuttles, waiting for them. Dr. Steinberg, a sturdy-looking woman with blunt features and light brown hair, was speaking to him in clipped whispers.

Data got the distinct impression that the two officers didn't intend for the cadets to hear their conversation. But of course, he couldn't help it.

"Whose crazy idea is *this?*" asked the doctor. "Saddling us with a bunch of cadets on an away team?"

31

The first officer grunted. "Not mine," he whispered back. "The captain seemed to feel they could use the seasoning."

Dr. Steinberg shook her head. "Seasoning's for when you're not operating under a deadline. I'm going to have to have a talk with our fearless leader when this is all over."

Sierra smiled. "For all the good it'll do. You know how stubborn she gets."

The doctor snorted. "Well, I can get pretty stubborn myself."

Data was not surprised by Steinberg's lack of confidence in him and his fellow cadets. He hoped that by the end of their mission, the doctor would have a different view of them.

Then the cadets were almost on top of them, and Steinberg and Sierra had to terminate their conversation. The first officer inspected each of his charges in turn, making sure their suits were sealed properly and their communicators functioning.

"All right," he said, once he was satisfied everything was in order. "Everybody knows what our mission is, right? We take a look around, locate the aliens that populated the station, and effect their rescue, if possible. Unfortunately, we don't have time to engage in a full-scale investigation of the place. Just in and out as quickly as possible. Got it?"

Data watched Cadet Majors. When he nodded, the android nodded, too. Then they entered the shuttlecraft and took their places in the seats provided for them. Within a matter of moments, Commander Sierra had moved them through the bay's force field and out into the void of space.

Peering past Sinna, who was seated in front of him, Data saw their objective through the forward observation port. The station was less than three kilometers away—a short trip, even for a shuttle.

Glen Majors was in the seat across the aisle from the android. Data observed him for a moment, but the human didn't return his glance. He was obviously too intent on what was ahead of them. The other cadets, scattered about the cabin, were silent as well.

Before long, the android could make out something that resembled a bay door in the hull of the alien station. Apparently, the first officer had noticed it as well—with the help of his sensors, perhaps—because he was piloting them in that direction.

Data could also discern a webwork pattern of small projections on the station's hull at intervals of less than a meter from one another. It was logical to assume that these were designed to provide handholds for exterior repair crews.

Of course, in dealing with an unfamiliar culture, one had to remember that appearances could be deceiving— or so Data's instructors at the Academy had warned him. In the present instance, for example, what looked like a bay door might have turned out to be something else entirely.

However, as the shuttle closed in, what looked like a door slid aside . . . and revealed itself to be a door, in fact. The chamber beyond it was big enough to house the *Republic*'s shuttle and several more like it.

"Seems at least one system on that station is still up

and running," commented Dr. Steinberg. She turned to look back over her shoulder at the assembled cadets. "That means we may find life support still functional as well."

Commander Sierra guided them in through the open doorway. No sooner had they touched down on the surface inside the station than the doors slid into place again, closing them off from the vacuum of space. And a second later, there was a soft *whoosh*—the sound of atmosphere flooding the chamber, Data guessed.

"How is it?" asked the doctor.

The first officer shrugged as he consulted his instrument panel. "Looks breathable," he noted. "Acceptable temperature, too . . . and gravity is point nine eight percent of Earth-normal. If it weren't for the radiation problem, we probably wouldn't need our suits at all."

"But there *is* a radiation problem," Steinberg responded, "so we'll keep them *on.*" She eyed each of the cadets in turn. "Won't we?"

They all agreed that they would. Then Commander Sierra opened the hatch in the side of the shuttle and stepped out to look around. A few moments later, he gestured for the rest of them to follow.

In less than a minute, they were all standing outside the shuttle, looking around the alien chamber. If it had ever been used as a vehicle bay, it was empty now— except for their own vehicle, of course.

The bulkheads here were white, like the exterior of the station. And the cone pattern was repeated on them, though only in the minutest detail. To the human eye, Data was certain, the bulkheads looked almost perfectly smooth.

"All right, people," said the first officer. He pointed to the bulkhead to the right of the shuttle, where the outline of a door could be seen rather easily. "Let's move out and—"

Before he could complete his instructions, the deck bucked savagely beneath their feet, throwing them all to the ground. All except Data, of course—and even *he* had trouble keeping his footing under such adverse conditions.

Then, as quickly as the incident had begun, it was over. Normalcy was restored. Picking themselves up, the android's biological companions gazed warily at one another and at their surroundings. However, there was no repeat of the strange and sudden quake.

"What was *that?*" asked Cadet Petros. She was rubbing her elbow, on which she seemed to have fallen.

"Good question," replied Commander Sierra. "My guess is that the station's propulsion system isn't entirely disabled after all, and that curve it just threw us is one of its fits and starts."

Sinna looked at the first officer. "Then we can expect that sort of thing again," she noted.

It wasn't a question, but Commander Sierra answered it anyway. "I'd say it's a good possibility, yes. So let's stay on our toes."

Dr. Steinberg sighed. If the frown on her face was any indication, her discussion with the captain would be even more heated than she'd originally intended.

The first officer, on the other hand, didn't show any outward signs of being daunted by the tremor. With a wave for the rest of them to follow, he led the way to the bulkhead with the door in it.

Like the door in the hull of the station, this one slid aside at their approach, revealing a corridor beyond. Commander Sierra walked up to it, poked his head out, and looked both ways. Then he stepped through.

Data caught a glimpse of Glen Majors as the rest of them filed out of the open doorway. The second-year cadet seemed as calm and confident as the first officer. Only his eyes moved, taking in sights that no Federation citizen had seen before.

Once everyone was out in the corridor, the android could see that it followed a gently curving path in either direction. Which way would they go?

Dr. Steinberg scanned the place with her medical tricorder. Judging by her expression, the results were not promising.

"No evidence of life signs whatsoever," the doctor announced, her voice flat with disappointment. "Though the radiation is making it rather difficult to obtain a reliable reading."

"It may be that there are no life signs to read," Cadet Petros pointed out. Then, noticing the looks of disapproval her remark had prompted, she added, "Of course, for the time being, we'll naturally assume otherwise."

They still hadn't decided which direction to take in negotiating the corridor. It was Commander Sierra who finally came up with a plan to address that problem.

"We'll split up," the first officer announced. "Majors, Data, Sinna, and Petros, you're with Dr. Steinberg. Everyone else is with me." He thought for a moment. "We'll meet back here in half an hour, tops. And sooner, if necessary."

"If necessary?" echoed Data.

37

Sierra regarded him. "If there's another quake, much worse than the first," the human explained. "Or a series of them." He took in the rest of them with a glance. "Anything that looks too dangerous for us to handle."

"In any case," the doctor added, "we'll stay in communicator contact, so there won't be any real judgment calls. Right, Commander?"

The first officer nodded. He pointed to one end of the corridor. "Good luck," he told his fellow officer.

"Thanks," she tossed back at him. "You, too."

Then, as Commander Sierra and his chosen team departed, she turned to her own charges. The android looked at her expectantly.

"Well," said Dr. Steinberg, "here's where the *real* fun begins. Shall we?"

"Certainly," replied Data, though no one else uttered a word, including Majors. As his fellow team members started down the corridor, he realized that he had answered a rhetorical question. Yet *again*.

He would have to be more careful to avoid that in the future.

CHAPTER

Data would have expected that, after several minutes, the curving corridor they were following would have intersected with some other corridor or produced something like a turbolift. As it turned out, it did neither of those things.

Nor did it produce any sign of the station's occupants. Finally, Dr. Steinberg couldn't help but take note of the fact.

"Still no trace of the owners," she observed. "Doesn't exactly inspire confidence, does it?"

"Maybe they had to cluster together to escape the radiation," Sinna suggested. "Some parts of the station may be shielded from it better than others."

The doctor nodded judiciously. "So you're saying the survivors are all hiding somewhere, and we just haven't stumbled across them yet. That could be, I suppose. And believe me, the physician in me hopes you're right."

"But we won't know for certain," Majors reminded them, "until we find some of them."

Dr. Steinberg looked at him. "That's true as well. I just wish they were a bit . . ."

Data never heard the end of her sentence. He was too busy focusing on the faint sounds coming from the stretch of corridor just ahead of them. The faint *scraping* sounds.

Sinna must have noticed some outward indication of his concentration, because she asked, "What is it?"

The android shook his head. "I cannot say with any degree of certainty," he replied. "However, I believe something or someone is moving toward us along the corridor."

The doctor shot a look back over her shoulder, but there was nothing there. Neither a sound nor any other sign of the station's occupants. Turning to Data again, she asked, "Are you sure you heard something? It wasn't your imagination?"

"Technically, I do not have an imagination," the android informed her. "Of course, it *is* possible for my auditory circuits to suffer a malfunction, but in this instance, I do not think that is the case."

"Wait," said Petros. As she glanced past Data, her dark brows came together in concern. "I just heard something myself. Like a . . ." Her voice trailed off ominously.

"A growl," supplied the android, finishing the thought for her. After all, he had heard it too. Even as he spoke, he heard a third such sound. And a fourth.

By then, it seemed, the entire team had heard because

40

their heads had snapped around and their eyes were focused on the corridor.

The growling grew louder. And *closer.*

Majors's eyes narrowed. "We've got to get out of here . . . fall back, review the situation. There's no point in endangering ourselves unnecessarily. We may be the only hope for the people on this station."

Data looked at the cadet, more impressed then ever. And Majors was right, wasn't he? If something happened to the away team, the station's aliens would *never* be rescued in time to avoid the super-Jovian planet ignition.

Apparently, the doctor agreed as well. "Come on," she said, beginning to retrace her steps. "We're going back the way we came . . . at least for now."

Just then, the android heard another round of distant growls—but not from the corridor up ahead. This time, it was coming from *behind* them.

"I am not certain that that would be a wise course of action," he advised Dr. Steinberg.

She looked at him quizzically. "Why not?"

"Because," he explained, "unless I am mistaken, the same organisms that are ahead of us are also behind us."

As the growling up ahead of them grew louder, the doctor's mouth became a thin, hard line. "You're right," she confirmed. "I hear them, too." She looked around for a moment, then grunted with frustration. "Looks like we've got only one option—my *least* favorite one. Set your phasers on light stun and follow me."

There was a series of rasping sounds as they drew their weapons and set them according to Steinberg's instructions. Then, satisfied that everyone was prepared, the doctor started back along the corridor in the direction of their shuttlecraft.

The growling—from both directions, but in particular from ahead of them—grew louder and fiercer with each passing second. Data stole a look at Majors, who seemed every bit as determined and focused as before. Taking heed of the cadet's example, the android held his phaser ahead of him and readied himself for whatever they might encounter.

Even so, he was surprised by the suddenness with which they were attacked. Before he knew it, the corridor was full of what looked like two-legged lizards— large, powerful creatures with scaly yellow skin and slitted purple eyes.

The doctor was barking orders at the cadets as they tried to catch up to the darting lizard forms with their phaser beams. Data only heard snatches of her words over the din of their adversaries' deep-throated snarls.

". . . back to back . . . break formation or they'll . . . that it's just practice . . . each shot count . . ."

After their initial confusion was over, the cadets began to connect with their targets. But the phaser blasts didn't seem to faze the lizard beings. And once they realized that, they came on with renewed fury.

"Heavy stun!" cried Dr. Steinberg at the top of her lungs, and the cadets tried to do as she told them. But there was no time—the lizard creatures were all over them, pounding and clubbing them with their fists, gouging and slashing at them with their claws.

The raw brutality of the assault took its toll on the android's companions. Sinna took a blow to the head and crumbled. Majors was slammed into a bulkhead. Pe-

tros's arm was wrenched up behind her, forcing a scream out of her, and the doctor was lifted high into the air, where her antagonist glared at her with saliva dripping from its maw.

Data didn't wait to see what the lizard creature had in mind for Dr. Steinberg. Bringing his superhuman strength into play, he grabbed the arm that held the physician aloft and, with his other hand, slugged his scaly adversary across the mouth.

The impact was enough to make the lizard being release Dr. Steinberg and recoil. But a moment later, as the android caught the medical officer in his arms, the creature recovered and leaped for his throat.

Sweeping Dr. Steinberg behind him, Data caught one of his opponent's wrists and whipped him toward a bulkhead. Had he taken the time to watch the lizard being's progress, he no doubt would have seen it hit the metallic surface and slump to the deck.

But he *didn't* have the time. He was too busy bracing himself for the attack of two other creatures. He fended off the first of them with a backhanded smash. The other managed to get a sharp-clawed grip on his arm.

The android was about to take hold of the lizard being by the scruff of its scaly neck and fling it away when he was filled with a sensation unlike any he'd ever known. It was as if a powerful electrical charge was running through him, savaging the workings of his neural net, disrupting his most basic functions.

Even as Data sank to his knees, no longer in control of his own limbs, he realized that the electrical emission had come from the creature holding on to his arm. Of course, it had no way of knowing how effective its emission would be, or that it would disable him a thousand times more surely than any brute force the lizard beings could have brought against him.

Taking note of his helplessness, another creature jumped him. And another. Unable to defend himself, he could only watch as they tore at his containment suit, and speculate as to what it would be like when they got past it and began tearing at *him*.

Abruptly, one of his antagonists was thrown clear of him. The other two were ripped loose as well, in quick succession. Incapable of even turning his head, the android could only see a trio of bright, red phaser beams crisscrossing in the air above him. And by that, he knew that all wasn't lost quite yet.

Apparently, his efforts had bought his comrades some time—enough to adjust their phasers to a higher setting, which was proving somewhat more effective against the lizard beings. Lying faceup on the deck, Data observed the creatures' abrupt departure out of the corner of his eye.

In a matter of only a few short moments, the corridor was clear of them. The only ones left standing were Dr. Steinberg and the three human cadets. Kneeling beside the android, the medical officer ran her tricorder over him. She seemed pale and her hair was in some disarray, but her concern for him seemed to override any of her other worries.

"What happened to him?" asked Sinna, not even bothering to try to disguise the anxiety in her voice. "He seemed to be doing fine, and then . . ." Her voice trailed off ominously.

Dr. Steinberg frowned. "I don't know enough about

him to make any kind of detailed diagnosis. However, it seems he suffered some kind of electrical shock—one that was powerful enough to upset the delicate electronics in his artificial nervous system."

Data was unable to speak or he would have confirmed her findings. As it was, he wouldn't have had time to do so because a moment later, he heard the same sort of growling that had alerted them to the lizard beings' attack.

"It's them again," announced Petros. She turned to the medical officer. "What do we do?" she asked.

Dr. Steinberg cast a troubled glance in the direction of the growling sounds. "We go the other way," she decided.

But there was no guarantee that that way wouldn't be full of lizard beings soon as well. Perhaps it already was, the android reflected.

"Wait," said Sinna, apparently thinking along the same lines. She pointed to what seemed to be an access panel in the bulkhead. "If this station is like one of our ships, it's got a network of tubes going through it for maintenance purposes—one that we can use as an alternative to the corridors. And that looks like a way in."

The medical officer looked at the panel, then at the Yanna, and then at the panel again. "There's only one way to find out," she reasoned. And without any further comment, she proceeded to the panel and attempted to work it free of its place in the bulkhead.

The thing came out with surprising ease. The open space behind it was quite suggestive of a tunnel. It seemed increasingly likely to Data that Sinna's theory was correct.

Turning back to the cadets, Dr. Steinberg pointed to the android's prone form. "Majors . . . Sinna . . . pick Data up and follow me in. Petros, you bring up the rear."

As Sinna bent to the task, Cadet Majors hesitated. "Sir," he said, addressing his comment to the medical officer, "is it wise to try to take Data with us? He'll slow us down considerably, and I doubt the lizard beings can do anything to him that they haven't already done."

The android didn't take the statement personally. He weighed it from an objective standpoint and came to the conclusion that Majors was probably correct in his assessment of the situation.

However, Dr. Steinberg shook her head. "No," she said firmly. "Data's one of us. And we don't leave our people behind, android or otherwise."

Majors looked as if he would have liked to press his case, but there wasn't time. The growls were getting louder again. Picking up Data by his arms, the second-year cadet waited for Sinna to lift the android's lower half. Then, when they had him securely, they brought him over to the opening in the bulkhead.

"He's a lot heavier . . . than he looks . . ." breathed Majors.

Sinna no doubt thought so as well. But she didn't say it. She just gazed down at Data with that worried expression. Perhaps she was right to be worried, the android mused. After all, no one knew when—or even *if*—he could be repaired.

Inserting Data into the opening, Majors and Sinna crawled in past him. Then, with the Yanna and the second-

47

year cadet dragging the android behind them, Petros pulled the panel back over the opening.

Immediately, the party of five turned right and made its way along what looked like the inside of a long, white cylinder, perhaps two meters in diameter. The thing seemed to stretch for a long way in either direction.

"Petros," called Dr. Steinberg, her voice echoing in the confined space. "I want you to scan the tube behind you for those lizard creatures. I'll do the same up here."

"Aye, sir," said Cadet Petros.

"Anything?" asked the physician.

"Nothing here in the tube," returned Petros. "But I'm reading several of them moving through the corridor on the other side of the bulkhead. Eight of them, to be exact. All together, like a pack."

Data heard Dr. Steinberg mutter something beneath her breath. Then, more loudly, she said, "I'm picking up a bunch of them out there, too. I'd say we'd be doing ourselves a favor by getting out of this area as soon as possible."

But she didn't take her own advice—at least, not right away. Tapping her communicator, the medical officer called for Commander Sierra, no doubt to warn him about what they had encountered.

There was no answer.

She tried a second time.

Again, no response.

That meant one of two things, Data decided. Either the radiation was preventing Dr. Steinberg's communication from going through . . . or something had happened to the first officer's half of the away team. For the time being, there was no way of knowing which set of circumstances had prevailed.

Apparently coming to the same conclusion, the doctor gave up on warning Commander Sierra for the moment and started off along the length of the tube. The others followed, with Data in tow.

As they proceeded, the android caught an upside-down glimpse of Glen Majors's face every now and then, whenever his head lolled in the right dirction. The cadet was scowling at him, no doubt displeased at having to expend precious energy on what must have seemed to him to be a lost cause.

The android regretted being a burden. If he could have spoken, he would have said so. As it was, he would have to endure his helplessness in silence.

"Petros," called Dr. Steinberg. "How long have we been on the station?"

There was a pause. "A little more than an hour," came the response. "Less than five hours to go before the super-Jovian planet ignition," Petros volunteered, obviously seeing through to the reason for the medical officer's question.

Five hours to the super-Jovian planet ignition, thought Data . . . and the end of their mission, if not their lives. After all, if they didn't get back to the shuttle in time, they and the rest of the station would be destroyed when the planet became a sun.

No sooner had that grim notion crossed his mind than he felt the fingers on his right hand twitch. Focusing his attention on them, he felt them move again—this time, at his command.

Was it possible that he was regaining control of his

body? That the effects of the electrical charge that had disabled him were only temporary?

"Data!" gasped Sinna, her eyes wide. She turned to look at Dr. Steinberg, who was up ahead of her. "I think he *moved.*"

A moment later, they stopped dragging him. The medical officer's face loomed above his as she ran her tricorder over him.

"I do believe his situation's improving," she commented thoughtfully. She leaned close to the android's ear. "Can you hear me, Data?"

The android tried to speak. "Yes," he croaked finally. ". . . hear you."

Steinberg smiled encouragingly. "I think," she said, "the situation is very *definitely* improving."

CHAPTER 5

By the time the group reached another access panel leading to the corridor outside, Data had pretty much recovered. His reactions were still a trifle slower than they normally were, but he had full use of all his limbs, and he could speak normally again.

"You know," said Sinna, as they waited for Cadet Petros to scan the hallway for lizard beings, "I thought that might have been the end of you back there." Her expression was clearly one of relief, with no sign of the resentment she had displayed for him over the past few days.

The android returned her gaze. "I thought it was the end of me as well. Fortunately, my system proved more resilient than either of us anticipated."

"There's no one in the corridor—at least, not for fifty meters in either direction," reported Petros.

Dr. Steinberg nodded approvingly. "All right. We

should be far enough along now to take our chances out there. But first . . ."

Tapping her communicator, she called for Commander Sierra. As before, there was no response. Apparently, the radiation was a barrier to communications in this area as well.

"Oh, well," she said, attempting to make light of the situation, though her concern was unmistakably etched in her face. "I guess we're still on our own, aren't we?"

"It would be nice," Majors remarked, "if we had some idea of where these creatures came from. They're obviously too primitive to be the aliens who sent the Mayday signal."

"Yes," agreed Petros. "Or, for that matter, to have staged an invasion of the station. So what are they?"

Data turned to her. "I have been pondering that question myself," he confessed. "It is possible that the lizard beings began as live cargo . . . kept in some sort of containers, perhaps. When the station collided with the asteroid, these containers may have been damaged, allowing the creatures to escape."

"An interesting theory," allowed the medical officer. "Though until we find some evidence to back it up, it's not much more than that."

"Right now," Majors noted, "the more important question is who *did* send the signal and where *are* they? All dead, destroyed by the creatures? Or just hiding from them in another part of the station?"

Even before he could complete his question, Cadet Petros was scanning the area for nonlizard life-forms. Given their failure to locate the station's inhabitants earlier, Data didn't expect any positive results.

Nonetheless, there was a faint smile on Petros's face as she looked up from her tricorder. "I think I found some of them," she told the others.

"Where?" asked Dr. Steinberg.

The cadet focused her attention on her tricorder again and used her free hand to point. "Over there," she said, indicating a point almost directly beyond the access panel.

The android and his companions looked at one another. "What are we waiting for?" asked the medical officer. "Let's go."

Cadet Majors removed the access panel. One by one, they slipped out of the tube that had been their salvation—first Data, then Sinna, then Petros and Steinberg. And when the last of them had emerged into the corridor, Majors put the access panel back in place.

"This way," announced Petros, intent on her tricorder again. She made a left turn and walked purposefully down the corridor.

The android saw Cadet Majors look around warily, so he did the same. Even though their scan hadn't turned up the presence of any lizard beings, Data knew it was advisable to remain alert.

A moment later, however, they reached their destination: a pair of large, silver doors set into the bulkhead. Together, the doors made up a perfect semicircle.

"For a while there," Dr. Steinberg commented, "I was beginning to think this place didn't *have* any entrances or exits—just an unending series of corridors."

"Do you think they open like the doors to the shuttlebay?" asked Sinna, taking a step closer to them.

As if in answer to her question, the silver surfaces slid

53

apart, revealing a room beyond. The Yanna muttered something beneath her breath as she led the way inside. It wasn't long before the others followed, with Data bringing up the rear. No sooner had he crossed the threshold than the doors slid closed behind him.

The place was much larger than the android had expected. Enclosed in a huge, transparent dome that made it seem open to the stars, it contained an impressive variety of trees, shrubs, and flowers arranged in a neat and orderly fashion.

Plant life was everywhere in thick profusion, each specimen distinguished by a different color and shape and texture. Some of them displayed flowers or leaves and some had more exotic appendages, but all were recognizable as living, growing flora.

"What do you think this is?" asked Petros, turning as she looked around. "Some sort of botanical garden?"

Data would have answered in the affirmative, but he didn't want to take a chance on being wrong. Majors already had seen him at his most useless; he didn't want to expose any more of his flaws by supporting the wrong conclusion.

"I wouldn't be surprised," said Dr. Steinberg with a confidence the android wished he felt as well. "After all, many of *our* stations have gardens. Why not *this* one?"

Majors wiped away some of the moisture that had gathered on his faceplate and brushed it on the shoulder of his containment garb. "Glad I'm wearing a suit," he remarked offhandedly. "You could do the backstroke in this soup."

The android tried to picture such an activity, but he

couldn't. Apparently, Majors's remark wasn't meant to be taken literally.

"No sign of the occupants," Majors went on, taking the immediate vicinity in with a glance. "But according to our instruments, they're here somewhere."

"What's that?" asked Sinna. A few steps ahead of the group, she pointed to something that the rest of them couldn't see.

Approaching his friend, Data followed her gesture to a short, squat tree with feathery, yellow filaments growing out of it and saw part of a *boot* sticking out from behind its trunk.

"There's somebody down this way," barked the Yanna for the benefit of the others. She knelt as she got closer to her objective.

The android, who was right behind her, saw that the unconscious, humanoid form was representative of a race he had never seen before—one with pale yellow skin and large oval eyes. The alien's eyes were closed now, his face in repose.

As the rest of the team gathered around Sinna's find, Dr. Steinberg ran her medical tricorder over him. Her brow wrinkling, she considered the results.

"Radiation fever?" suggested Majors. "Or maybe an attack by one of the lizard creatures?"

The doctor grunted. "Certainly not an attack. There are no wounds, no broken bones, not even so much as a bruise. But it's not radiation fever, either."

Another possibility occurred to Data. "Is it possible that this is a natural response to dangerous environmental conditions?" He blurted it out before he had a chance to think twice.

Dr. Steinberg looked up at him. For a long, uncomfortable moment, the android was certain that she would dismiss his idea as ridiculous.

"Actually," she said, "that's just what I was thinking. Some species withdraw into an apparently comatose state as a way of protecting themselves. I've got a feeling that this is one of them."

Sinna scanned the place. "There were supposed to be others here. And if they're all in this condition . . . with those lizards running loose . . ."

"They are fortunate they were not set upon and killed," Data noted, completing her statement.

It was only afterward that he realized he need not have done so. Sinna's sentence fragment was sufficient to convey her meaning.

"Fan out," instructed the doctor. "See if you can find the rest of them."

Even before she finished, Data was on the move. His search had only gone on for a few seconds before he spied another of the now familiar boots. It was protruding from the fringe of a spiky, orange thicket.

"Dr. Steinberg," he said, "I have located a second alien." He pointed as he started toward it. "Over here."

"Make that three," responded Petros, who was moving in a different direction entirely. "No, wait . . . it looks like a *couple* of them."

"I've got one, too," called Majors, who was pursuing still a third course.

"Bring them all over here," the doctor told them. "It'll be easier to take care of them if one of the lizards somehow finds his way in."

Before long, they had collected all the aliens into a single area of the garden—the same location where they'd discovered the first one. There were five of them in all, three males and two females, each as pale and insensible as the next.

Sinna shook her head. "They must have thought this was a good place to take refuge—from the lizard creatures, I mean, not the radiation."

But Dr. Steinberg wasn't listening to the Yanna, it seemed to the android. She was still sitting on her haunches and running her tricorder over the aliens, apparently intrigued by something she had yet to share with them.

Finally, she leaned back and grunted. "How about that?" she said.

"What is it?" asked Majors.

"I thought I saw some similarities in the basic skeleton," the doctor replied, "but the DNA patterns confirm it. Our friends here and the lizard beings seem to represent two branches of the same family tree."

"You mean they're . . . related?" asked Petros, unable to conceal her surprise.

Dr. Steinberg nodded. "Looks that way. Not all that closely, mind you, there could be millions of years of evolution separating them."

"In much the same way as the Terran ape and modern homo sapiens," Data observed.

"Yes," the doctor agreed. "An apt analogy." She sighed. "So what does that tell us? That both these aliens and the lizard beings came from the same planet. . . ."

"That these people must have known what they were transporting," concluded Petros, "but felt secure with whatever safeguards they'd built in."

"True," Dr. Steinberg confirmed. "And that the collision with the asteroid, not to mention the ensuing radiation, put a wrench in their plans."

"But we still don't know why they were carrying this kind of cargo," Majors reminded them. His jaw muscles worked. "And we're no closer to securing the help of the natives than we were before."

Petros eyed the doctor. "Is there any way to revive them? Maybe just enough to get some answers?"

Steinberg shook her head. "Dangerous and inadvisable. We don't know enough about their physiology to try and bring them out of their comas—and that won't change until I can get them to sickbay."

"There are quite likely others like them on the station," Data offered tentatively. "The ones who sent the distress call, for instance. Perhaps *they* can supply us with the information we seek."

"Unless," said Petros, indicating the beings at their feet, "it was *these* people who sent the distress call."

Majors nodded once in terse agreement. "And even if it wasn't, the corridors are still full of lizards." Again his jaw muscles fluttered. "Talk about dangerous and inadvisable. We make one wrong move and we're history."

The android was considering Majors's viewpoint when something happened—something quick and violent and too powerful to resist. The next thing Data knew, he was picking himself up off the floor and watching the others do the same. The android was unharmed, but his companions were nursing bruises and even a few minor abrasions.

They had fallen victim to another quake, he observed, just as Commander Sierra had predicted they might. And this one was worse than the one they had experienced earlier.

"Figures," moaned Petros, holding her arm and wincing in pain. "The same darn elbow."

"Sir," said Majors, as he helped Dr. Steinberg to her feet. "If you recall, Commander Sierra told us we were to return to the shuttlebay if the quakes got much worse or if we encountered some other danger. At this point, I'd say that both those things have happened."

The physician nodded as she brushed herself off. "Normally, Mr. Majors, I'd agree with you—except we've found what we're looking for." It seemed to Data that there was a harder line to Steinberg's jaw now. "And that changes everything," she finished.

CHAPTER

6

The doctor frowned. "The way I see it, it's up to us to save these people, now that we know where at least some of them are. There are two possible ways to do that. We can try to evacuate the station gradually, taking a chance each time that we'll be caught and destroyed by the lizard beings. Or we can take a shot at moving the station away from the radiation source—allowing the *Republic* to beam off our team, Commander Sierra's team, and—if possible—both sets of aliens."

She licked her lips. "My preference, of course, would be the latter option. Like any Starfleet officer, I hate the idea of allowing any life-form, even a hostile one, to be destroyed. Unfortunately, to save both the occupants of the station and the lizard beings, we would have to have the expertise to operate the station and some assurance that the thing is still navigable, which it may not be. A long shot, at best."

Data replied before he could think better of it. "I can obtain the expertise to operate the station," he said.

Everyone looked at him. "You can *obtain* it?" echoed Cadet Majors. His eyes were slitted. He sounded skeptical, to say the least.

The android nodded. He already regretted having spoken so boldly, but it was too late to retract his statement.

"Yes," he confirmed. "I can *learn* to operate the station. After all, my positronic brain is essentially a computer. It should not be all that difficult for me to communicate with the computer on the station. Once that link is established, I can determine if the navigation and propulsion systems need repairs, repair them if they do, and attempt to operate them if they do not."

Dr. Steinberg appeared interested. "This linking up with the station's computer..." She paused. "You couldn't do that from here, could you?"

"I would need to reach the station's operations center," Data replied. "That is the place most likely to offer such access."

Majors was shaking his head. It seemed to the android that this was a gesture of derision intended to question the credibility of Data's remarks. A moment later, this observation was confirmed.

"We're talking about an android—a mechanical man—running an entire station," Majors pointed out. "And an alien station, at that." He looked at the doctor, at Petros, and finally at Sinna. "Oh, he can probably learn a few things by hooking up to its computer. But operating a facility this size takes more than knowledge, it takes instincts." He glared pointedly at Data. "And that's one thing our friend here is lacking. In fact, he'd probably be the first to admit that."

The android had to concede the cadet's point. "That is correct," he said. "I have no instincts. Or at least, none that I am aware of."

"Wait a minute," interjected Sinna. "Data's got more instincts than he gives himself credit for. A few weeks ago, he took charge of a Federation ship called the *Yosemite*—a ship that he came aboard knowing nothing about. If he could do that, maybe he can run this station as well."

Majors grunted. "From what I understand, he lived on a Federation ship for *years* with nothing to do but educate himself. Is it any wonder that, after all that time, he knew how to run that particular kind of vessel?"

The Yanna's blue streaks darkened. "I suppose you were there then?" she blurted. "I suppose—"

A *growl* stopped Sinna dead in her tracks. It was exactly the kind of sound they'd heard just before they were attacked by the lizard beings.

Glancing in the direction of the doors, the android saw that they were still closed. *Besides,* he thought, *I would have heard them if they had opened.*

Yet there was a lizard creature in this room with them. And, judging by the sound it had made, it was somewhere nearby. Hidden in the profusion of alien foliage. About to *pounce.*

Then, before Data could locate it, the creature showed itself. Bolting from cover, it flung itself at Cadet Petros with such blinding speed that neither human nor Yanna had a chance to react.

Fortunately, the android was a little quicker than his

companions. Hurtling across the intervening space, he managed to grab hold of the lizard being's shoulder and drive it off its mark.

It was only as the creature rounded on Data that the android realized what a chance he had taken. The last time he had recovered from the lizard beings' electrical charge. This time he might have been incapacitated forever.

Still, as the creature coiled to leap at him, Data held his ground. He had a responsibility to protect his team, after all, just as they would have protected him if their roles were reversed.

However, as luck would have it, there was no need for his resolve to be put to the test. Before the lizard being could strike, a ruby red phaser beam caught it full in the chest and sent it flying back into a soft bed of purple blossoms.

It didn't move again. Its scaly chest barely rose and fell with the rhythm of its breathing.

Glancing back over his shoulder, the android saw that it was Sinna who had taken the creature down. Her phaser was still in her hand, aimed at the lizard being as if she expected it to resume its assault at any moment.

However, that seemed unlikely to Data. As he approached the creature, it became increasingly obvious that Sinna's close-range blast had subdued it.

"Careful," warned Dr. Steinberg, who had a phaser in her hand as well. She was looking all about them, peering into the thick foliage like a bird whose sense of self-preservation had been stirred. "There could be more of them."

But Petros shook her head. Holding up her tricorder

as evidence, she said, "It doesn't look like it, sir. At least, not at the moment."

"How did it get *in* here?" asked Majors. It was difficult, even for an android, not to hear the tension in his voice or to see the pallor that had taken over his face.

Data wondered why Majors's reaction was more intense than that of the doctor or his fellow cadets. If the android didn't know better, he would have concluded that the human was succumbing to a fear response. However, this was Glen Majors, a proven model of confidence. *Surely,* Data told himself, *there has to be another reason for the human's appearance.*

"That's a good question," said Steinberg, in reply to Majors's question. "Until we know the answer, let's keep our phasers out and our eyes peeled." She took out her tricorder. "In the meantime, I'm going to take a look at our uninvited guest here."

Complying with the woman's orders, the android took out his phaser and helped stand guard. However, that didn't stop him from glancing over his shoulder from time to time.

Without a hint of hesitation, the medical officer walked up to the unconscious lizard being. It only took a few seconds to scan the scaly body, but Dr. Steinberg lingered a lot longer than that over the results she saw on the tricorder's readout.

"Interesting," she noted at last. "It appears there's a blockage in one of the creature's glands."

"Does that have some special significance?" Data inquired.

The physician looked up at him. "Hard to say," she answered. "For all I know, it's *supposed* to be blocked."

As the android absorbed this information, he continued to examine their surroundings for some sign of additional lizard beings. After a second or two, his search took him past the collection of unconscious station occupants lying side by side on the ground.

Even a human would have been hard-pressed not to notice that something had changed among the occupants. Something rather significant, in fact. "Dr. Steinberg," he said.

The medical officer turned to him. "Yes, Data?"

"It seems," he reported, "one of the aliens is *missing*."

Dr. Steinberg's reaction was one of incredulity. "That's not possible," she responded. "We would have noticed. . . ."

Crossing the room under the cadets' watchful gaze, she counted the unconscious forms herself. As the android had pointed out, there were four of them, not the five that had been there only a little while ago. The medical officer looked around, no doubt wondering how they might have misplaced an entire sentient being.

"Lord," she said finally, yielding to the evidence of her own eyes. "You're right, Data. One of them *is* missing."

Suddenly, Sinna snapped her fingers, a habit she had picked up from her human peers in her short time at the Academy. "One of the aliens vanishes . . ." she said, leaving the comment hanging in the air.

The android followed her gaze as it shifted meaningfully to the other side of the room . . . where the lizard being was still prone in a bed of purple flowers. Abruptly, Data understood.

"An alien vanishes and a lizard creature appears," he remarked, finishing Sinna's thought for her.

"No," muttered Cadet Majors, as he considered the possibility and summarily rejected it. "It's got to be a coincidence."

However, Petros seemed not to have heard Majors. Her brow wrinkling as she peered at Data, she asked, "Are you saying . . . ?"

The android nodded, anticipating the remainder of her question. "Indeed," he said, "I am. As bizarre as it sounds, it may be that the lizard being who just attacked us was an unconscious alien a scant few seconds earlier."

Dr. Steinberg grunted softly. "I'll tell you what. That would go a long way toward explaining the presence of the lizard creatures on the station. They could *all* be aliens who first went comatose and then somehow regressed into primitive, savage versions of themselves."

"But why," asked Petros, "would they pick *this* particular time to undergo their metamorphosis?"

"It could be an effect of the radiation," Data suggested.

The doctor nodded. "Maybe that blocked-up gland I found in the lizard being is supposed to control the aliens' metabolism. When working properly, it keeps the aliens in their evolved state—and when not working normally, it allows them to devolve into beasts."

"That could be it," agreed Sinna. "After all, no race would venture into space if it expected to change into a pack of primitive creatures halfway through its travels."

Steinberg turned to Petros, who had become their unofficial timekeeper. "How long have we been here?" asked the medical officer.

The cadet's reply was quick and accurate. "Two hours

67

and forty-seven minutes, sir. A little more than three hours until planetary ignition."

Steinberg looked dubiously at the four remaining aliens. "Under the circumstances," she began, "I think we can rule out the possibility of evacuating these people. Otherwise, we might find that we're carrying unconscious aliens one minute and savage lizard creatures the next."

"So we head for the—"

Before the cadet could complete her statement, the station lurched again. It wasn't as bad as the second time, but it was vicious enough to cut their legs out from under them again.

As the first one up, the android offered to help Dr. Steinberg to her feet, but she waved him away. "I'm getting rather tired of this," she announced. Brushing a stray lock of hair out of her eyes, the medical officer turned to Petros. "You were saying?"

Petros shrugged. "It looks like we've got no choice but to look for the operations center," she concluded.

Sinna nodded. "It's the only real option open to us, isn't it?"

Cadet Majors looked at her. "I don't think so," he said calmly.

CHAPTER
7

As the android looked on, Cadet Majors turned to Dr. Steinberg. "Sir," he asked, "are you absolutely certain you want to venture out there? We'll just be casting about, trying to figure out where the operations center is. In the meantime, we'll be fair game for every creature on the station."

The doctor eyed Majors for a moment, no doubt considering his point of view in light of his stellar reputation at the Academy. "Believe me," she said at last, "I've thought about that. But if we're to rescue these people, we've got to take some chances."

Then, without any further discussion, Steinberg headed for the door. Data saw Majors's frown deepen before—grudgingly, it seemed—he fell into line behind the medical officer.

The android wondered if Cadet Majors might not be right. After all, he'd had more training in tactical matters. The doctor had been thrust into the role of leader, even though it was clearly not her field of expertise.

As Data weighed this possibility in his mind, he saw something out of the corner of his eye. A streak of yellow-green, darting from one clump of foliage to another.

One of the lizard-creatures, he thought. Drawing his phaser, the android waited for it to show itself again.

"Data," said Steinberg, stopping to look at him. There was a note of alarm in her voice. "What is it? Did you see another of them?"

"Yes," the android replied, careful not to take his eye off the spot where he believed the creature had hidden itself. "Or perhaps it is the first one we found, recovered now from Sinna's phaser beam."

"Leave it here," the doctor told him. "We're going to be gone in a minute anyway."

"With all due respect, sir," Sinna responded, "it could follow us out into the corridor. Better to deal with it now and not have to worry about it later."

"Besides," added Petros, "it could hurt the aliens."

Another officer might have taken offense at the cadets' audacity. However, Dr. Steinberg seemed to be the kind of person who valued the opinions of others, no matter who they were.

"All right, then," said the medical officer. "We'll do as Cadet Sinna advises. But once we've stunned it, we're out of here." She licked her lips, her eyes flitting from one section of the botanical garden to another. "Whatever you do, stay together. I want everybody's back covered." A pause. "Lead on, Data."

The android did as he was told. Advancing between

two clumps of alien flora, he looked right and then left. Still no sign of the creature, no flash of scales to give it away.

Suddenly, Majors cried out, "I've got it!"

At the same time, a crimson beam sliced through the air, tearing apart a spidery shrub with black leaves and yellow flowers. As the ruined leaves fluttered to the ground, the cadets all converged on the spot.

But there was no lizard being there. Everyone looked at Majors, who looked back at them with something like anger in his voice.

"I thought I had it," he barked. His face darkened until it was the same color as his phaser beam. "I don't understand how I could've—"

Data was too distracted to fully grasp what happened next. However, the result of it was painfully obvious, especially to Dr. Steinberg—who found herself grappling desperately to keep a hissing lizard creature from ripping out her throat.

Majors aimed his phaser at the lizard being—but before he could fire, Petros pushed the weapon aside. "You'll hit the doctor!" she cried.

Noting the wisdom in Petros's warning, the android realized that there was only one other option open to him. Once again, undaunted by the possibility of having his neural net destroyed, Data flung himself at the creature and tore it free of its hold on Dr. Steinberg.

Then, reluctant to set it loose, the android slammed the lizard being to the ground. He didn't dare use his full strength, for fear of killing it. But the impact was sufficient to daze it for a moment.

That was all the time the other cadets needed. Two

71

phaser beams hit the creature, one right after the other, and the lizard being went limp in Data's grasp.

Turning his attention to Dr. Steinberg, the android saw that she had been badly hurt. Though her containment suit was uncompromised, the skin around her right temple was already purple with large, painful-looking bruises. There was a good chance she had suffered internal injuries as well.

"Data . . ." she groaned, through clenched teeth. "My hypospray . . ."

Locating the device on the outside of the doctor's suit, the android detached it and handed it to her. With trembling fingers, Steinberg input the necessary information and pressed the spray against her upper arm, where it injected her right through the fabric of the containment suit with the compound she had prescribed.

A second later, Data saw the medical officer relax. The muscles in her face seemed to lose their tension as well.

"A painkiller," Steinberg breathed, providing an explanation. "Making me groggy . . . so groggy . . . but necessary." Raising her hand, she gestured for the android to lower his face closer to hers. "Can't see well," she told him. "Or think well. But . . ." Her nostrils flared with the effort to stay focused. "I'll need medical help soon . . . if I'm to survive."

By then, the other cadets had clustered around them. Sinna and Petros winced at the sight of their fallen leader. Only Cadet Majors kept watch over the garden, so none of the other creatures could take them by surprise.

"What would you have us do?" the android asked the doctor.

Steinberg swallowed. "Take me someplace . . . someplace *safe* from the creatures, Data. Then head for . . . for . . ."

Before she could finish, her eyes closed and her head lolled to the side. Concerned, the android used his tricorder to measure her bio-signs.

The doctor was unconscious but stable. Unfortunately, there was no guarantee that she would remain that way.

"What was she trying to tell us?" asked Petros. "What did she want us to do after we took her to a safe place?"

"The same thing she asked us to do before," Sinna replied. "Find the operations center and see if we can maneuver the station out of the asteroid belt."

The Yanna looked to Glen Majors, as if expecting him to oppose her, as he did earlier. However, the second-year cadet wasn't even looking at her. He was staring at Dr. Steinberg, paler than ever.

Data approached Majors, though the human didn't seem to notice. "Are you all right?" he asked.

Finally, Majors turned to him. But he didn't answer. He just clenched his jaw, turned back to the medical officer and went on staring.

It took them a while, but the cadets finally found what Dr. Steinberg had asked them for: someplace safe. A cabin that was free of the lizard creatures and likely to stay that way.

The search might have gone faster, but as they progressed through several different corridors and maintenance tubes, they were forced time and again to elude the lizard beings prowling throughout the station.

Several times, Data's tricorder had warned him that they were close to being cornered by the creatures. But in each instance, the cadets had managed to slip away without actually encountering them.

Sitting with their backs propped against the cabin's walls and the motionless figure of the medical officer stretched out between them, the android and his companions took a moment to think things through.

"One of us has to stay here with Dr. Steinberg," Sinna said after a while, "while the rest of us try to locate the operations center."

Abruptly, Cadet Majors—who had been silent and unresponsive until that point—shook his head. "No," he stated flatly. "We're not going to the operations center. We're staying right where we are until help arrives."

Majors looked even paler than before, Data observed. And he was sweating much more profusely than either Sinna or Petros.

Petros looked at the second-year cadet, a little surprised. "But Dr. Steinberg told us she wanted us to—"

"Dr. Steinberg isn't in charge of this mission anymore," Majors pointed out. "*I* am. I have seniority here. And *I* say we stay where we are."

It was true that Majors outranked them, the android reflected. However, he had learned at the Academy that a standing order from a commanding officer was to be carried out no matter what—even in that officer's absence.

He said so.

"Wait a minute," said Sinna, smiling at Data. "That's

right, isn't it? We have to follow Dr. Steinberg's instructions, no matter who outranks whom."

Majors swallowed hard. "Listen to me," he told them. His voice was reedier than normal. "It's too dangerous to try to reach the operations center. For one thing, we still don't know where it is. And even if we find the place, our friend the android may not be able to accomplish as much as he thinks." He licked his lips. "Our best bet is to stay put until the captain sends another team after us."

Data was as reluctant as ever to question Glen Majors's judgment. Of all of them, Majors had the most experience in such scenarios—at least in terms of Academy simulations. And besides, every account of him that the android had ever read described Majors as outstanding leadership material.

And yet . . .

The android straightened. "I do not think 'staying put,' as you describe it, is the best course of action," he remarked. "If we wait too long, Dr. Steinberg could die here. Also . . ."

Data hesitated. After all, this was Glen Majors he was talking to. Glen Majors, who had not so long ago been the standard of confidence to which he aspired.

But somehow, he couldn't be certain anymore that the standard was still valid.

"I may be more capable than you give me credit for," he finished.

Majors seemed taken aback, at first. Then he glared at the android, his eyes narrowing, a cruel smirk taking shape on his lips.

"How about that," he said slowly. "The mechanical

man thinks he knows more than *I* do." The muscles worked in his temples for a moment. "All right, Data. You want to show us how smart you are, go ahead."

The human got up and crossed the small room, then looked down at Data from his full height. He pointed a forefinger at the android—a forefinger that was trembling with barely contained emotion.

"But *I'm* still the one in charge," rasped Majors. "I'm still the leader here. And when your little plan turns sour, *I'll* be the one who'll have to figure out a way to get us out of here."

For thc first time, Data recognized that Sinna might have been right about Glen Majors. The android didn't know much about leadership, but even he understood that a good commander was not supposed to let his emotions get the best of him.

Perhaps, he told himself, *Cadet Majors is not such a good role model after all.*

CHAPTER

It turned out to be a simple matter to track down the alien station's operations center. Data just had to follow the bundles of circuitry in the tubes they'd been traveling through all along.

Where the bundles became thicker, it stood to reason that they were getting closer to their destination. Where the bundles became thinner, they were getting farther away.

"And you knew this all along?" asked Sinna, as they crawled through a tube, just ahead of Cadet Majors. Despite Majors's earlier statements, he was showing no particular desire to lead them.

"I did not *know* it," the android corrected her. "I simply suspected. Even now, there is no proof that I am correct in my assumption—though I believe we will know that soon enough."

"You mean we're almost there?" asked the Yanna. She seemed understandably relieved by the prospect.

"Based on my estimate of the station's size," Data replied, "I would say we are not more than three hundred meters from the operations center. If we do not reach it in the next several minutes, we will know that my hypothesis is without a basis in fact."

"And then we'll have to start all over again," Sinna noted.

The android nodded. "Yes, an inconvenience, though a significant one. However, for Dr. Steinberg, such a state of affairs might prove disastrous."

Petros had volunteered to stay and watch over the medical officer. However, the cadet knew almost nothing about how to care for Steinberg. As the doctor herself had pointed out, she needed the sort of facilities only the *Republic*'s sickbay could offer.

Abruptly, Data stopped and looked back over his shoulder, in Majors's direction. The second-year cadet, who was crawling with his head down, didn't notice the android's action. But Sinna did.

"What is it?" she asked the android.

Data listened with all the concentration he could muster. A moment later, his effort was rewarded—if one could call the distant sound of *growling* a reward.

"The creatures," he told his friend. "I hear them coming." He pointed past Majors, back in the direction they had come from. "From that direction," he elaborated.

"The creatures?" echoed Majors, suddenly roused from his reverie. He stared hollow-eyed at the android. "We can't let them get to us in here. We won't have a prayer in such close quarters."

Data returned his gaze. "I do not think we have a choice," he responded. "There are no exits in sight. I suggest that you and Cadet Sinna get behind me and keep moving. I will do my best to protect all of us."

"No," the Yanna told him, her expression solemn and determined. "I'm not going to let you sacrifice yourself for us."

The android took out his phaser and made sure it was set on heavy stun. "I have no intention of sacrificing myself," he told Sinna. "There is simply no room in this tube for more than one of us to establish a defense. And as the one able to fire the fastest and with the greatest accuracy, it seems reasonable that I should act as rear guard."

It was not easy for the Yanna to argue with that. Clamping her lips shut, she crawled past Data. Majors was right on her heels, obviously not eager to remain in the creatures' way.

By the time his fellow cadets were up ahead of him, the growling had grown louder. And within seconds, Data caught a glimpse of the foremost creature as it came hurtling toward them along the length of the tube.

Carefully, the android took aim and fired his phaser. Its fiery red beam hit the lizard being square in the chest. As it slumped to the bottom of the tube, two more appeared in its wake.

Data was able to take one of these down, but not the other—at least, not right away. And as he made the attempt, two new creatures bounded past the unconscious forms of their pack-mates.

What followed was difficult even for the android to follow. Even as he disabled several of the lizard beings with his stun beams, a few others appeared to skitter past him by virtue of their great speed. By then, it

seemed, Sinna and Majors had entered the fray as well, discharging their phasers with whatever accuracy they could manage in the narrow confines of the tube.

It was bedlam. Chaos. Data found himself wrestling with one of the creatures. No sooner had he slammed it against the lining of the tube, knocking it senseless, than another leaped at him.

But fortunately for the android and his companions, the conflict didn't last very long. When the tube was quiet again, and Data counted nine unconscious lizard beings in all, none of the cadets had been hurt very badly, though their containment suits had been torn here and there.

The android's suit, in particular, had suffered several long gashes. However, it had not been in good repair even before this battle. His previous confrontations with the creatures had taken their toll on it.

"Just great," said Majors, inspecting a small rip in his garb. "How long am I going to be able to tolerate that radiation now?"

"I would not worry about that if I were you," Data told him. "By the time the radiation becomes a problem for you, the super-Jovian worlds will have become a sun. At that time, we will either be safe back on the *Republic* or destroyed in the process of ignition."

Majors cast a withering look at the android through his faceplate. "Thanks," he muttered. "I feel a whole lot better now."

"Come on," said Sinna. "Let's get out of here before a few more of them get wind of us."

This time, Majors scurried ahead of them. And though he continued to look back over his shoulder every so often, he set an admirable pace. But after they'd followed the tube for fifty meters or so, they encountered the last thing Data had expected.

A dead end.

At least, for the three cadets. The bundles of circuitry continued through a tiny hole in the barrier ahead of them, presumably into the operations center proper. However, the android and his companions couldn't have hoped to fit through that hole in their wildest dreams.

"I can't believe this," snarled Majors. Frustrated, he pounded his fist on the barrier. "We've come all this way and for what?" Turning to Data, he spat, "You said you would get us to the operations center!"

"I said I would try," the android replied. "And I have not yet given up on the attempt. Nor did I expect that this tube would lead us all the way into the facility we seek."

"We passed an access panel just a couple of minutes ago," Sinna offered hopefully. "If we're in the neighborhood of the operations center, we ought to be able to reach it via one of the corridors."

Majors's eyes opened wide. "The corridors? But there's no telling how many of them could be out there."

"If they're in the tubes," the Yanna observed, "we're not safe anywhere. Don't you see that?"

"We would've been safe if we'd stayed in the cabin with Steinberg and Petros," Majors argued. "We never should have left that place."

"It is too late for this discussion to gain us anything," Data reminded them. And without another word, he headed back toward the access panel they'd left behind.

Sinna had the sense to follow him. And without anyone to contend with, Cadet Majors had no other option but to trail along.

It only took a few moments for Data and his comrades to find the access panel, exit the tube, and make their way through the corridor to a set of doors. Like the doors to the botanical garden, they opened with a soft hiss at the cadets' approach.

But as those same doors closed behind them, the android observed that they were not in the place they had been looking for. Judging by the look on Majors's face, he had come to the same conclusion.

"This isn't an operations center," he said, walking across the room toward its only console and scanning the monitor on the bulkhead above it. "It can't be. It's too small, too sparsely equipped." He cast a withering glance at Data. "You blew it, Tin Man. *Again.*"

The android conceded inwardly that he had miscalculated. They seemed to be in a specialized facility of some sort—one with its own small airlock, no less. He guessed that it was an environmental control nexus or something similar, but definitely not an operations center. However, there was no point in dwelling on that now. He could ponder his failings later.

If there *was* a later.

At this moment, Data told himself, the preferred course was to assess their situation and see what steps were required to reach the goal they had set for themselves. Advancing to the console where Majors stood, the android took a closer look at the monitor.

It displayed a cross section of the station, rendered in thin, blue lines. There were red and green dots at intervals, perhaps signifying life-support stations. Using his forefinger, Data started with their point of entry and traced the path they had taken through the alien facility.

"What are you doing?" asked Sinna.

"Attempting to determine our present location," he explained. A moment later he found it. "We seem to be *here*," he noted, indicating the spot for his companions' edification. "If I am correct, we are near the middle of the station."

"And the operations center?" asked the Yanna.

The android moved his finger to the representation of a somewhat larger cabin than the one they occupied. "That would appear to be *here*," he told her. "Approximately one hundred meters away."

"Sure," spat Majors, the muscles working in his jaw. "Lead us on another wild goose chase. And how are we supposed to get there *this* time?"

Frowning at Majors, Sinna went over to the airlock hatch and hunkered down beside it. "Too bad we can't get around *outside* the station."

Too bad indeed, Data agreed silently. Unfortunately, their containment suits weren't proof against the rigors of space, and since they had been ripped in the latest lizard attack, they were even less so.

The android's head tilted as something occurred to him. Knowing what that meant, Sinna approached him.

"You've thought of something," she said.

"I have," he admitted. "Specifically, that one of us *can* have some mobility outside the station."

"That one being you," Sinna noted.

"Precisely," Data replied. "After all, the station is not moving through space. And since I do not require air to breathe, or a strictly controlled environmental temperature range, I can survive for a limited period in the vacuum. Certainly, long enough to make it to the next airlock."

"Which conveniently opens on the operations center?" asked the Yanna.

"I do not believe so," the android answered, glancing again at the diagram of the ship on the alien monitor. He pointed to what he believed was the location of the next airlock. "However, it appears to open on a facility just down a short corridor from it."

Sinna looked at him. "And if it doesn't?"

"Then I am risking no other life but my own," Data assured her, though it was, the android gathered, not the answer she was hoping for.

"Wait a minute," snarled Majors, drawing his companions' attention. "You're not really going to do this," he told Data.

"Why not?" asked the android. If the cadet had a valid reason that prevented him from proceeding with his plan, he wanted to hear it before he went any further.

"Because I made this trip to humor you," Majors continued. "I never had any intention of letting you try to pilot the station out of the asteroid belt." His eyes narrowed in what Data now recognized as contempt. "You're not a pilot," the cadet rasped. "You haven't got the instincts or the experience. All you'll do is get us killed."

Data looked at him. "Nonetheless," he said resolutely, "it is the only way to save the station and its occupants—ourselves included."

Believing that their conversation was over, the android moved to the airlock—until a bright, red beam of light speared the bulkhead just ahead of him, leaving a smoking, black char mark on the metallic surface.

"Data!" cried Sinna.

Data turned and saw the phaser in Majors's trembling hand. It was pointed right at the android. And at this close range, it was highly unlikely that it would miss.

CHAPTER 9

"I told you you're not going anywhere," said Cadet Majors. He swallowed hard. "Now step away from the airlock, both of you, and there won't be any trouble."

The Yanna did as she was told. But Data just tilted his head. There was only one way to ensure their survival—that much was clear to him. How was it possible that Majors did not understand that?

"This is not a logical response," he told the human. "Time is running out. Not just for Dr. Steinberg, but for all of us."

"No!" shouted Majors.

Taking a step toward the android, he narrowed the gap between them even more. Majors's free hand clenched into a fist. "There's plenty of time for Captain Clark to figure out what's happened. She'll send someone after us. And we'll be out of here before the planet ignites."

"Perhaps," Data conceded. "But there is no guarantee of that. And even if the captain manages to get *us* off the station, there almost certainly will not be enough time to remove the occupants . . . or the lizard beings." He paused. "Or to give the doctor the care she needs."

But Majors was shaking his head back and forth—much too quickly for anything the android told him to sink in.

"No, no, *no*," he groaned. "We can't try to pilot ourselves out of here. We've got to wait for the captain. That's the only way we're going to get off this station alive."

As Majors went on with his tirade, he seemed to have

forgotten about Sinna. She had noticed and was starting to take advantage of the situation by gradually circling around behind him.

However, the Yanna wasn't in position yet to knock Majors down. And if he realized what she had in mind, he might do to her what he had done to the bulkhead. Data had to make sure that didn't happen—and the only way he could do that was to keep Majors focused on *him*.

The ability to deceive was not one of the android's strong points. In fact, he was not equipped for it at all. But in this case, Data would have to try to exceed the limits of his programming. He would have to try to cover his friend's actions or see her skewered by Majors's phaser beam.

"Er . . . let us say you are correct," the android told the upperclassman. "Let us say the captain does rescue us from our predicament. What will she say about the way we conducted ourselves? What report will she make about our failure to help everyone else on this station?"

Majors's eyes opened wide as he considered the possibility. "You're right," he murmured. "Everything I've worked for . . . all these years . . . it'll go down the drain. I'll be drummed out of the Academy."

With each word, Sinna was getting closer to her destination. But she still wasn't there yet.

Abruptly, Majors's eyes brightened. "Unless . . . she doesn't find out what happened." He smiled crookedly at Data. "And she won't . . . if there's no one to tell her about it."

"What do you mean?" asked the android.

"What I mean," the upperclassman explained, "is that the

survivors write the history books. You would've learned that in your Academy classes if you'd survived long enough."

"Cadet Majors," said Data, "you must think about what you are doing. You must ask yourself if it is worth taking a life merely to salvage your career in Starfleet."

The upperclassman nodded. "It's worth it, all right. Besides . . . you're not really alive. You're just a bucket of bolts that *thinks* he is. And as for your friend the Yanna . . ."

As soon as Sinna came to mind, Majors seemed to guess what was going on. Whirling, he found her directly behind him, about to strike. But with his phaser aimed at her midsection, he was in a position to strike first.

And he almost certainly would have, if not for Data's inhuman quickness. Reaching out, he grabbed Majors by the left shoulder and spun him around, so that his phaser beam cut a black swathe in the bulkhead instead of Sinna. Then, with his other hand, the android took hold of the upperclassman's wrist and squeezed with just a fraction of his great strength.

Unable to hold on to it, Majors watched the phaser fall to the deck with a clatter. In a flash, Sinna had darted over and snatched it up. Only then did Data release his fellow cadet.

As soon as he was free, Majors threw a punch at him. The android hadn't expected that, but he saw it coming in time to move his head to the side and avoid it. He ducked a second swing as well. Then, with the utmost care not to injure the man, Data thrust him toward one of the bulkheads.

Majors rounded on the android, his face a tortured

91

mask of emotions that Data could not begin to interpret. "You tricked me!" he barked.

"Yes," said Sinna, smiling grimly as she pointed the upperclassman's phaser at him. "Pretty good for a mechanical man, wouldn't you say?"

The irony wasn't lost on the android, though he chose not to comment on it. "If you will watch over Cadet Majors," he told the Yanna, "I will proceed into the airlock."

Sinna nodded. "Good luck, Data."

"Thank you," the android told her. Then, pulling open the airlock door, he crawled inside and shut it behind him. A couple of meters ahead, he saw the outer door—the one that led to the vacuum of space.

Pulling out his tricorder, he checked the time. There wasn't much of it left. It had been four and a half hours since they left the *Republic*. In another fifty-five minutes, they would all be incinerated—unless his plan worked.

Data put his tricorder back in its place and made his way to the outer door. It opened just as the inner door had, with a slight pull. The android stuck his head out into the starlit vacuum of space.

There was no mistaking the fact that the station was surrounded by asteroids. However, the one it had crashed into wasn't visible from Data's vantage point, no doubt because of its location on the other side of the facility.

He could see the line of raised handles that ran between two of the station's large, white cones—from the airlock to a point somewhere beyond. That point, though difficult to locate right now, was his destination—the operations center.

Pulling himself out of the airlock, Data latched on to the first of the handles and began the most unusual journey he had ever undertaken.

The android couldn't help but remark inwardly on the still and entrancing quality of the void. It was not like scanning the heavens through an observation port, he reflected. He wasn't standing on the deck of a ship or space station and gazing out into space, all the while remaining separate and aloof from it.

At this moment, it seemed to Data that he was *part* of space—that he had been fully integrated into a larger plan, a celestial drama that most beings never knew. It surprised him that he should perceive it to be so, and yet he did.

But the biggest surprise of all was the awesome spectacle of the impending super-Jovian planet ignition. Painted on such a large canvas, it was so compelling . . . so extraordinary . . . the android had to make a conscious effort not to pause and stare at it.

The larger of the two gas giants—the one that would actually blaze into life as a new sun—was a dusky orange color, with bands of silver and brown drifting through it. The smaller gas giant was a light blue throughout. And between them, where their warring gravities were bending light and other energies, Data could discern twisting filaments of bright crimson.

All in all, quite intriguing, quite engaging. Though Data had no feelings per se, he had long ago recognized in himself the ability to appreciate beautiful things, and this was certainly the most beautiful phenomenon he had ever been privileged to see.

What would Captain Thorsson of the *Tripoli* say if he could see the android now? After all, Thorsson was the one who had encouraged Data to join Starfleet in the first place. It was the only way, the captain had told him, that he would be able to satisfy his enormous curiosity about the universe.

And after just a couple of weeks, he was doing just that.

Of course, he could take little comfort in the fact. He still had to reach the station's operations center, and as quickly as possible, before the spectacle of the converging gas giants became a scene of destruction. Turning away from the two planets, he concentrated as hard as he could on the task ahead of him.

Making use of handhold after handhold, he pulled himself along the skin of the alien station. It did not require much effort, given the lack of gravity. In fact, a child could have accomplished it, providing that he or she was able to survive out here.

As he proceeded in this fashion, the next airlock came into view. With his goal in sight, the android began to think about what he would do once he reached it. Fortunately, he still had his phaser. Otherwise, he might have had to punch a hole into the hatch in order to gain access to the interior space beyond it.

Data had barely come to this conclusion when the metal surface beneath him shuddered noticeably. Just in time, he tightened his grip on the handholds—because a moment later, the station bucked savagely beneath him, almost throwing him off.

It continued to buck, like some rabid space-beast, each motion more violent and vicious than the one before. The android could only cling to the station's hull, his cheek pressed against its cold, hard surface, and hope that the strength of his android limbs was equal to the task at hand.

Still, he had the presence of mind to seek out the cause of the quakes. Just over the horizon to his left, Data could see the distant blue gleam of thrusters on the other side of the station.

Apparently, Commander Sierra had been right in his assessment of the situation. The station's propulsion system was active but damaged in some way. Unfortunately, if it was moving the facility at all, it was propelling it deeper into the asteroid belt.

And in the process, the android was forced to wage the struggle of his brief life. Somehow, he had to hang on. If he failed, he knew, he would be sent pinwheeling out into the emptiness of space.

And once Data was out there, he would have no way to propel himself back; nor was it likely the *Republic* would find him in time. He would simply drift through the void until the super-Jovian world ignited. And not even an android could expect to survive a conflagration of that magnitude.

These were the images that came to mind as Data fought to maintain his hold on the station. They made him even more determined to ride out the tremors. And if the prospect of destruction weren't enough, there was the knowledge that he was the only hope for Sinna and the others.

A few seconds later, however, the vibrations subsided and finally vanished altogether. Spurred by the knowledge that they might start up again at any time, the android made his way across the remaining distance as quickly as he could.

In a matter of a few short minutes, he reached the airlock.

CHAPTER

10

Taking out his phaser, Data adjusted the setting so that it would provide a tight beam and sufficient force to spring the latches on the airlock cover. Then, aiming it with almost surgical precision, he activated the device.

A tiny red beam sprung out of the phaser's emitter array and vaporized the latch. Moving over, he did the same thing to the next latch, and the next. Then he replaced the phaser in the pocket reserved for it in what was left of his containment suit. Finally, with great care, he grasped the edge of the airlock cover and pulled.

The hatch swung up easily on its hinges, with no hint of a complaint. Bringing his legs around in front of him, the android slipped down inside the airlock. Then he closed the cover behind him and used his phaser to weld it shut.

Making his way from one end of the airlock to the other, Data wrestled open the inner hatch. Then he inserted himself through it until he emerged into the space beyond. Looking around in the soft yellow glow of the emergency lighting, the android saw that he was in another cargo bay. And unless he had made a horrible miscalculation, the entrance to the operations center would be just down the corridor.

Wary of meeting a lizard creature or two, Data took out his phaser again. Then, the doors yielding as he approached, he stepped out of the cargo bay and looked around.

No lizard beings. But there was another set of doors. With no time to waste, the android darted toward them. As they opened, they revealed a large chamber.

Data took it in with a single, sweeping glance. Had he been human, he would have breathed a sigh of relief because this was clearly the alien station's center of operations.

The ranks upon ranks of monitors were proof of that. Most of the monitors were alive, indicating that the station's systems were still largely operational.

Unfortunately, the eleven individuals who were slumped over onto the control consoles were anything *but* operational. They were of the same race as the aliens the android had found in the botanical gardens—and just as unconscious. A quick scan with his tricorder revealed to Data that there were no lizard creatures in hiding; though, given how little he knew about the transformation process, that might only be a temporary condition.

His tricorder was also able to act as a chronometer, telling him how much time he had left. *Twenty-two minutes,* thought the android.

Only twenty-two minutes . . . and then the super-

Jovian planet would burst into solar flame. Would it be enough?

Data's first priority was to clear the operations center of the senseless aliens. Spotting a small room off the main area, he carried the aliens inside and locked them in by melting the door controls with his phaser. Then he turned his attention to the various station monitors.

The only question then was whether he could do what he said he could do: pilot the station out of the asteroid belt. Without another moment's hesitation, the android applied himself to his self-imposed assignment.

First, he familiarized himself with the computer system's protocols. Then he asked the computer to display all the categories of information he would require in order to pilot the station.

It was more than Data had expected. Then again, the level of technology on the station was somewhat more primitive than that currently in use by the Federation—and more primitive systems generally required more expertise to operate.

Unfortunately, the assimilation of that expertise would take a while. But there was no other option at hand. All the android could do was follow the lightning-fast scroll of information across the monitors in front of him and do his best to keep up.

By the time he was finished, another twelve minutes had gone by. The super-Jovian world would ignite in slightly more than ten minutes, he remarked inwardly. Touching the station's helm controls for the first time, he ran them through a diagnostic cycle. Fortunately, everything checked out all right.

Data could maneuver the station all right; the only

problem would be thruster power. Based on what he had seen during his climb out in space, the thrusters were only operating sporadically.

It didn't take long for the android to confirm that fact on his control board—at least as far as the starboard thrusters were concerned. The set on the port side was still in working order, it seemed.

Activating the port thrusters, Data began to withdraw the alien space station from the asteroid it had run into. It wasn't easy, considering how firmly certain parts of the facility had embedded themselves in the asteroid's surface. However, with a gentle nudge here and there, the android managed it.

Almost miraculously, there were no hull breaches. Though the station's outer skin had buckled in some places, it had not broken.

The next step was to maneuver the station out of the asteroid belt. That was a more intricate task. Some of the asteroids were so close together, they barely gave Data any margin for error. But somehow, he found a way to get through even the tightest squeeze.

In fact, he was almost done when he came to the narrowest passage of all. According to the android's calculations, he had no more than several meters' clearance on either side. Leaning just a bit closer toward the monitor ahead of him, he focused on the adjustments he would have to make in order to fit the station through the space provided.

Then he applied port thrusters—the only ones he could depend on—and started ahead. The station was halfway through when he heard a loud bang behind him and then a shrieking, as of twisting metal.

Allowing himself only the quickest of glances, Data saw that three of the aliens he had deposited in the next room had turned into lizard beings. And he had underestimated their strength, because they had managed to tear open the door he had welded shut.

The android didn't dare give the creatures any more of his attention. If he did, he would be running the risk of damaging the station or worse, jamming it into a place from which he couldn't extract it.

So when the first of the lizard beings tried to twist his head off, he grabbed it by its wrist and flung it into another control console, but he didn't look away from his monitor.

When a second one clawed at his arm, he backhanded it with all the power he could generate—sending it sliding back across the floor of the operations center, judging by the sound. But he didn't turn away from his monitor.

Even when the third one leaped on him, clamping its teeth down on his artificial neck, he didn't flinch. He simply pried the creature's jaws loose and pinned it down against a part of the console he wasn't using.

The lizard being hissed and slashed at Data's hand, trying to free itself. But he couldn't let it go. The station was almost free of the asteroid belt.

In the back of his mind, the android knew that the creature might destroy his neural net at any moment with an electrical discharge. But he resolved to expose himself to that risk, if that was what it took to complete his maneuver.

One of the station's cones scraped against the asteroid to port, hard enough for the contact to send a vibration through the operations center. Setting his jaw, Data ro-

tated the alien facility three degrees—just enough to avoid a second such incident.

The lizard being in his grasp writhed and spat, tearing at him with its feet as well as its hands, shredding what was left of his containment suit and much of the Academy uniform below it. But the android continued to ignore the creature. And a moment later, he was rewarded as the station slithered free of the asteroid belt.

The *Republic* was visible now, hovering just outside the belt, its hull gleaming in the lurid light of the imminent ignition. No doubt, the captain would be glad to witness the station's withdrawal.

Finally, Data was able to devote his attention to the lizard being. Standing, he picked it up off his console, removed his phaser from the dangling piece of fabric that had been his pocket, and fired at point-blank range. The creature went limp in his grasp.

Setting the lizard being down on the floor as gently as possible, the android applied himself once again to the duties of a pilot. With the asteroid belt behind him, he aimed the station for open space and called for best speed from the thrusters.

At the same time, he whipped out his tricorder and observed the amount of time he had left before the super-Jovian worlds collided. Had he been human, he would certainly have gasped.

Thirty-eight seconds.

Data calculated how far the station would have to travel in order to escape the ignition's effects. With an entire set of thrusters out of order, it would be close. *Too* close. Unlike the *Republic,* the alien facility wasn't built for speed. More than likely, it had been transported across interstellar distances by some sort of space tug.

On the other hand, the android thought, he might be able to build some leeway into the schedule. His study of the aliens' propulsion technology had shown him that there was a chance to increase the station's speed by recycling the plasma flow that provided its thrust.

Immediately, he set to work on the problem. When he looked up, the monitors showed him an increase in speed. Enough, he estimated, for all the station's occupants to survive the planetary ignition—at least in theory.

There were now only twenty-six seconds left before the super-Jovian world became a ball of intense, solar flame. All Data could do now was watch . . . and trust that his efforts to this point hadn't been for nothing.

Twenty seconds.

The asteroid belt began to fade into the distance. The *Republic* was running neck and neck with the station now.

Fifteen seconds.

The android glanced at each of the three lizard beings who had attacked him earlier. Fortunately, they were all still unconscious. None of the aliens in the next chamber seemed to be undergoing a metamorphosis, so there would be no problems from that quarter in the immediate future.

Ten seconds.

He tapped the communicator badge on his chest. "This is Cadet Data," he announced, "speaking to whatever Starfleet personnel still survive. Please brace yourselves. We are about to experience the shock wave from the ignition of the super-Jovian worlds."

Five seconds.

Four.

Three.

Two.

One.

CHAPTER 11

As the larger super-Jovian world collided with its smaller companion, the android felt a shudder in the deckplate beneath his feet—one that started out small and seemed to build in intensity until it became something massive and irresistible, and he was certain the station would be torn apart by the sheer power of it.

But it wasn't. Somehow, the alien structure managed to hold together, to weather a storm the magnitude of which its designers probably never contemplated.

As Data gazed at the rearview monitor in the operations center, he saw the waves of colored splendor that radiated one after the other from the meeting of the gas giants. For several minutes, nothing else happened.

Then, as if by magic, the combined mass of the two worlds began to erupt in a light so pure, so blinding, even the android's artificial eyes couldn't stand the sight of it. And when it was finished, only seconds later, the resulting object was a self-sustaining fusion furnace.

In other words, a star.

A new celestial body had come into being, Data reflected. A new pinprick of illumination in the night sky. And he had been on hand to witness it.

Abruptly, his reverie was interrupted—by the sound of a human voice. "This is the Federation starship *Republic*," stated the voice, "hailing the unidentified station. Please respond."

The android recognized the voice as that of the *Republic*'s communications officer. With the station now unhampered by the radiation produced in the asteroid belt, they were apparently able to converse freely again. He tapped his communicator badge again in order to reply.

"This is the unidentified station," he said. "Cadet Data speaking from the operations center."

"Data?" sputtered another voice, that of Captain Clark, he believed. "Is that *you?*" she asked.

The android confirmed that it was indeed *him*.

"What's the situation over there?" the captain inquired. "Where's Commander Sierra? And Dr. Steinberg?"

"Due to the radiation that permeated the station," Data replied, "I have not communicated with Commander Sierra since we first came aboard. And Dr. Steinberg is in need of medical attention, though her condition appeared to be stable when I saw her last."

There was a pause on the other end. Then, "Injured?" echoed Clark. "How did that happen?"

The android told her . . . about the quakes and the lizard creatures and his journey outside the ship. And about Cadet Glen Majors, whom Sinna was still holding at bay with the aid of a phaser, as far as Data knew. He related everything he thought the captain might want or need to know, remembering the captain liked things brief and to the point.

"Stay right where you are," Clark told him as soon as he was finished. "Now that we're out of the asteroid belt, I can send over additional teams to establish order there. And you don't have to worry about Dr. Steinberg. She'll be in sickbay in a matter of moments."

The captain was as good as her word. Data had hardly begun to remind her that he wasn't worried about the doctor—that he was, in fact, *incapable* of worry—when a couple of officers materialized in the aliens' operations center, both of them armed with hand phasers.

As soon as they were whole, the officers noticed the half-ruined door to the next room and the unconscious lizard creatures lying about. They looked at the android.

"Are *you* responsible for this mess?" one of them asked.

Data thought about all the lizard beings he had stunned in the course of his stay on the station. "Yes," he said. "This and a great deal *more.*"

Once free of the asteroid swarm, the lizard creatures began gradually to revert back to their original forms. According to a fully recovered Dr. Steinberg, the glands that prevented the aliens' metamorphosis were able to start functioning again once the radiation that had disabled them was no longer present.

What's more, the aliens—who called themselves the Umiiga—were so grateful for the *Republic*'s help in rescuing them and repairing the station, they offered to share any number of technologies with the Federation. Captain Clark's suggestion was that they apply for membership first, an offer the Umiiga promised to consider.

As for Commander Sierra, his group appeared to have fared somewhat better than Dr. Steinberg's. The first officer had his share of run-ins with the lizard beings as well, but his people avoided any serious injuries. Apparently, as time ran out for the station, they were on their way to the operations center as well, although Data beat them to it.

The android reflected on this information as the turbolift doors opened and he emerged onto the bridge of the *Republic,* followed closely by his friend Sinna and Cadet Petros. Some of the bridge officers grinned at them as they made their way to the captain's ready room.

Pausing, they waited for the door to open. Then they filed inside and came to stand before Captain Clark, who was seated at her desk, intent on the monitor that dominated it. It was a moment before the captain looked up and scrutinized each of the cadets in turn.

"I'd ask you to pull up a chair," Clark told them, "except I haven't got one for each of you."

However, Data mused, if the captain had asked them to "pull up a chair," he would have been clever enough not to take her literally. At least he had learned *something* during his brief stay at the Academy.

Clark leaned forward. "I'm going to make this short and sweet," she said. "What you did on that station was nothing short of brilliant. And more than that, it took guts." She turned to the android in particular. "I know

you're going to deny that you're *capable* of exhibiting guts, Mr. Data, but I'm going to beg to differ with you. And since I'm your commanding officer for the time being, I'd think twice about disagreeing with me."

Restricted from dissenting, the android said nothing. The captain smiled at him.

"Good move," she remarked.

A moment later, Clark's expression changed. It was as if a shadow had fallen across her features, Data noted.

"Unfortunately," she went on, "not everyone on your team displayed the qualities I would hope to see in a

Starfleet candidate. I think you know of whom I'm speaking."

Just for the record, Sinna said his name. "Cadet Majors, sir."

The captain nodded. "Yes. Obviously, he's going to be held accountable for what he pulled back there on the station. My guess is he'll be expelled from the Academy as soon as we return you to Earth." Clark sighed. "It's too bad. He was the most promising cadet we'd had in years. Everyone expected big things from him, myself included."

The android looked at Captain Clark. "Sir, is it possible that Cadet Majors's career can still be redeemed? Perhaps, given a second chance . . ."

Clark grunted. "Are you absolutely *sure* you're not human, Data? If I didn't know better, I'd say your emotions were showing."

"I did not speak from an emotional perspective," the android replied. "I only hoped to spare Starfleet the loss of a most promising resource."

That restored the smile to the captain's face. "We'll see," she said. "And in any case, that's not for us to decide."

"One thing puzzles me, sir," remarked Sinna. "With all the times Data was forced to grapple with the lizard creatures, why didn't he receive a second electrical shock from them?"

"Good question," Clark replied. "As it happens, I just learned the answer a little while ago. It turns out only the Umiiga males were capable of generating that kind of charge. And among the Umiiga, females outnumber males ten to one."

The Yanna nodded. "That makes sense. Thank you, sir."

The captain smiled. "You're welcome." Clark went on smiling a moment longer. Then she dismissed the three cadets with a backhanded gesture.

"Go on," she told them. "Get out of here. Thanks to you, I'm going to be up to my eyeballs in reports all the way back to Earth orbit."

Without further ado, Data and his companions turned and left the ready room. As they crossed the bridge, the android noted again how the officers there were grinning at them. *With approval,* he thought.

Commander Sierra turned in his chair. "Good going," he told them. "Any time any one of you wants a berth on a good ship, you just say the word."

"Thank you," said Data. Sinna and Petros expressed their gratitude as well.

As the android led the other two cadets into the turbo-lift, he noted that his attitude had changed somehow. He seemed to be taking all this praise in stride—as if he deserved it. As if he was reasonably certain that he could earn their praise again.

Could this be confidence? he wondered.

Petros accompanied them as far as deck five, where her quarters were located. Data's quarters, and Sinna's as well, were on deck seven.

As the lift doors closed, the Yanna looked up and smiled a tight smile at the android. "I told you so," she remarked.

Data tilted his head. "I do not understand."

"About Cadet Majors," she explained. "I told you he wasn't worth modeling yourself after."

"Yes," the android agreed. "You did." He thought about it. "It appears I was not very perceptive when it came to Cadet Majors."

"That's all right," Sinna went on, her grin widening. "Contrary to what Professor Pritchard may think, we *all* make mistakes."

Data had to concede that his friend was right. However, he resolved, he would try to make *fewer* of them as time went on.

About the Author

When roused (usually by his wife, Joan) from one of his frequent and enduring daydreams of a world where baseball players never go on strike and White Castle hamburgers grow on trees, Michael Jan Friedman will admit to being the author of sixteen books, including twelve *Star Trek* and *Star Trek: The Next Generation* novels (three of them collaborations with other authors). Mike additionally pens the *Star Trek: The Next Generation* and *Darkstars* titles for D.C. Comics (actually, he types them, but why split hairs?).

When he's not writing—a condition that occurs less and less frequently these days—Friedman enjoys sailing, jogging, and spending time with his adorable spouse and two equally adorable clones ... er, sons. He's quick to note that no matter how many Friedmans you may know, none of them is related to him.

About the Illustrator

TODD CAMERON HAMILTON is a self-taught artist who has resided all his life in Chicago, Illinois. He has been a professional illustrator for the past ten years, specializing in fantasy, science fiction, and horror. Todd is the current president of the Association of Science Fiction and Fantasy Artists. His original works grace many private and corporate collections. He has co-authored two novels and several short stories. When not drawing, painting, or writing, his interests include metalsmithing, puppetry, and teaching.